Don't Read This!
and Other Tales of the Unnatural

DON'T READ THIS!

and Other Tales of the Unnatural

Margaret Mahy—Charles Mungoshi
Susan Cooper—Roberto Piumini—Klaus Kordon
Eiko Kadono—Paul Biegel—Kit Pearson
Bjarne Reuter—Uri Orlev—Jordi Sierra i Fabra

illustrations by
The Tjong Khing

Front Street 8 Lemniscaat
Asheville, North Carolina
1998

Volume © 1998 by Front Street Books, Inc.
Previously published under the title *Lees dit niet en andere griezelver-halen* © 1997 by Lemniscaat b.v. Rotterdam. Stories: *Fingers on the Back of the Neck* © 1996 by Margaret Mahy; *The Mountain* © 1972, 1980 by Charles Mungoshi; *Ghost Story* © 1996 by Susan Cooper; *Don't Read This!* © 1996 by Roberto Piumini, written in Italian under the title *Attento a Te*, translated into Dutch by Vincenza Profita; *The Ravens* © 1996 by Klaus Kordon, originally published in German under the title *Drei Alte Weiber*, translated into Dutch by Tjalling Bos; *The Mirror* © 1996 by Eiko Kadono; *The Ivory Door* © 1996 by Paul Biegel, originally published in Dutch under the title *De Ivoren Deur*; *The Eyes* © 1996 by Kit Pearson; *Grandfather's Clock* © 1996 by Bjarne Reuter, written in Danish under the title *Farfars Ur*, translated into Dutch by Maydo van Marwijk Kooy; *The Song of the Whales* © 1996 by Uri Orlev, written in Hebrew and translated into Dutch by Mr. Herzberg; *Uninvited Guests* © 1996 by Jordi Sierra i Fabra, originally published in Spanish under the title *Cambio de Cerebro*, translated into Dutch by Piet de Bakker; all translations from the Dutch into English by Elisabeth Koolschijn.

Library of Congress Cataloging-in-Publication Data
Fingers on the back of the neck and other ghost stories
Don't read this! : and other tales of the unnatural
Margaret Mahy . . . [et al.] : illustrations by The Tjong Khing
p. cm.
Previously published under the title
Fingers on the back of the neck and other ghost stories.
Summary: An international collection of ghost stories
and spooky tales by such authors as Susan Cooper,
Roberto Piumini, and Bjarne Reuter.
ISBN 1-886910-22-7 (hardcover : alk. paper)
1. Ghost stories. 2. Children's stories. [1. Ghosts—Fiction. 2. Short stories.] I. Mahy, Margaret. II The, Tjong Khing, ill. III. Title.
Pz5466 1998
[Fic]—dc21 98-3215

Contents

Margaret Mahy

Fingers on the Back of the Neck

When Ivor was very small and walking down the jetty with his great-grandmother, May, he liked to feel her fingers resting against the back of his neck. "Oops!" she would cry, catching him if he stumbled over the rough boards of the jetty deck. But by the time he was eight, interested in computer games and completely determined to go to St. Christopher's, the most stylish school in town, her affectionate touch irritated him. And by the time he was twelve, and her long fingers were so much more arthritic and knobbly, he could scarcely bear it.

"I hate the way she strokes my neck when we're out walking," he complained to his mother. "I hate the way she says 'Oops!' as if it was *me* who was almost falling over, not her."

"Put up with it," his mother said. "It'll all be worth it one day. She just adores you, and she's simply loaded." She meant that Great-Grandmother May was rich.

Rich! At first it had seemed a fairy-tale word, like "magician" or "unicorn." But after a while May's thick, pale carpets, her heavy silver spoons, and the pictures on her walls began whispering to Ivor, over and over again. "Rich! Rich! Rich!" said these voices every time he came to call. If, for some reason, his father couldn't afford the fees for St. Christopher's, Ivor believed May would help out. His mother always said she would. It came as a shock to find that May actually disapproved of private schools. She might be rich, but she had no sense of style, and Ivor's mother said style was everything.

Saturday after Saturday Ivor would take the bus over the hill, heading for the lonely edge of the harbor where Great-Grand-mother May lived. And at some time during every long, boring Saturday afternoon, May would suggest a walk down to the edge of the sea and along the jetty.

Sometimes the tide was fully in and waves were breaking against the retaining wall. Sometimes Ivor and May would find themselves staring out over a great expanse of shining mud, with the sea a mere slot of cloudy green in the distance. But unlike the sea, the jetty did not change.

It was a long jetty, and as Ivor walked along it with May half a step behind him, he often felt that it was secretly stretching itself. Over all the weeks and months and years of Saturdays, he came to know it by heart. There was one thick plank with a twist in its cracked grain and a particular hollow knothole that seemed to wink at him as he stepped over it. Another gave off a curiously resonant *clonk* whenever he stood on it, and then a softer, less definite sound when he moved off again. Seagulls and, occasionally, kingfishers, perching on the worn jetty railings, would watch Ivor and his great-grandmother strolling toward them, then fly off at the last moment. The seagulls circled lazily, often coming back to perch on the jetty rail once more, but the kingfishers shot away, like jewels exploding over the sea.

"Are you rich, May?" Ivor had once asked her when he was small.

"Oh, I've got enough put aside for a rainy day," she had answered rather disapprovingly, as if the word "rich" was a sort of swear word. So he hadn't liked to ask her just how much she had actually managed to save, and what would happen to all that money when she died.

Sometimes he was allowed to put up a green tent in the scrambling garden and camp out all night. May did not camp with him, but she would sit at the door of the tent with a thermos of hot chocolate, which they shared as they listened to the snicker of possums challenging one another among the branches of the plum tree, or the shuffle of summer hedgehogs. It was strange, however, that the enclosed and shadowy garden had none of the mystery that seemed to hang over the open, sunlit jetty. Or perhaps the mystery was not so much *around* it as actually *in* it, seeping invisibly out of all the cracks of age and weathering in its old wood.

And *clonk!* The loose board always sounded its single note as he stepped on it, then sighed a little as he stepped off again. The rail always felt a little rough and splintery under his hand. And sooner or later, Great-Grandmother May, walking behind him rather more slowly than she had walked a few years earlier, would let her hand fall lightly and fondly on the back of Ivor's neck.

"The water's never quite clear . . . never *sparkling*," she once said. "But I've grown quite fond of this cloudy green. In a funny way it seems truer, because life's *cloudy*, don't you think?"

Ivor despised cloudy lives. He always thought of rich people as clear and sparkling. Rich people certainly preferred sparkling, sandy beaches, and though his parents always seemed to be struggling to make enough money between them, they tried to live like rich people. Each Christmas they rented a vacation house beside a real ocean, where there was no harbor mouth to throttle big waves and surf. Swimming in this sea, Ivor felt sparkling too. When these holidays were over and he and May walked along the jetty together, he would dream of that other sea, and of dry, white sand burning the soles of his feet.

"How did you get to be rich?" he asked his great-grandmother.

"I bought a piece of land some years ago," she said, "just

before Meg died." (Meg was her daughter, Ivor's grandmother. She and her husband had been killed in a car accident before Ivor was born.) "And then I sold it for a lot of money. But, really, I'm well-to-do because I live simply . . . I don't spend a lot."

"Mum says you're rich," said Ivor. "She says you could help us a lot more than you do."

May was silent for a moment.

"You probably know that I think your parents *waste* money," she said at last. "And I don't like waste. I look after money carefully, because one of these days I'll probably have to pay someone to look after me." She paused. "Oh, my goodness, what *has* happened here?"

An oval hole had been burned through the thick planks close to the jetty rail. It was still smoldering at the edges. Someone must have lit a fire on the jetty.

"Why would anyone do a stupid thing like that?" May said angrily. "Sheer vandalism!"

"It's burned right through," said Ivor. Peering into the blackened hole, he was fascinated to find the sea looking back at him. It was as if the jetty had suddenly grown an eye, black where human eyes were white, with a deep, shifty green pupil. It was an eye with the power to read minds. He sprang back from the hole.

"I don't think it's dangerous," May said. "I mean, I don't think it's likely to start burning again. But I'll ring the Harbor Board when I get home."

They reached the end of the jetty. The tide was in, and they walked down the steps to the very edge of the water.

"Be careful!" said May, as if he were still only a little kid of four. But Ivor barely heard her.

I looked into you, back there, the sea seemed to be telling him. *I saw what was in your heart.*

On their way home he took care to walk as far as possible from the burned eye, and by next Saturday the hole was patched over with a square of tin. It gave out a clashing note of its own when Ivor stepped on it, which he often did, grinding his foot hard down, because even though it was blinded, he knew the eye was still there under the lid, and that it always recognized his step.

By the time he turned twelve Ivor had mostly stopped visiting May, for, as he grew older, his parents began including him more and more in their own adventures.

"Let's *really* go away this Christmas," his mother said. "I don't just mean up north. Let's pop over to Oz . . . go to the Gold Coast. Have a wee gamble."

"Trust you to come up with a scheme like that," said his father, sounding both fond and irritated. "It hasn't been a great year, business-wise, and we'll have big school fees next year if Ivor goes to St. Christopher's."

"What do you mean, 'if'?" asked Ivor, suddenly alarmed.

"Well, nothing's certain in this life," his father replied. "I do my best, but I'm not *made* of money. And St. Christopher's—well, you know it's a very expensive school."

But Ivor's mother hooked her arm affectionately round his father's neck.

"All work and no play makes Jack a dull boy," she cried. "And Ivor and I don't like dull boys. We like cool Kit-cats." (Kit-cats were what the boys from St. Christopher's were often called.) "Anyhow, who knows? We might win enough to pay the fees ten times over."

"If I had a dollar for every time I've heard you come up with an argument like that, we'd be able to buy the whole school," said his father.

All the same they flew, business class, to the Gold Coast,

where the sea was sparkling and beautiful and there was plenty of warm sand. The beaches were crowded, but Ivor loved crowds. He realized that the lonely old jetty had always frightened him in some way. It had always made him feel it was about to reveal some terrible accident. Yet nothing terrible had ever happened on the jetty. May would certainly have told him if it had. Of course May loved him—Ivor knew that—but he knew by now that he didn't particularly enjoy love unless other good things went with it.

Halfway through the holiday, one of May's neighbors rang to tell them that May had had a bad fall. She was in a wheelchair, with neighbors watching over her and a district nurse calling in once a day. "It was a bad break," the neighbor told Ivor's father. "When are you coming home?"

"In about five days," said Ivor's father. "We'd come sooner, but you know what the holiday season's like. Every flight is booked solid."

When they did go back home, however, Ivor's father drove over to see May immediately. He came back looking sad and troubled.

"She's not too bad," he said. "Well, she's frail, but reasonably cheerful. However"—he looked at Ivor and his mother cautiously— "it might be a good idea for Ivor to forget about St. Kit's for a year or two."

Ivor and his mother cried out as if they had both been stabbed.

"No harm in going to a state school just for a bit, is there?" said Ivor's father.

"There's all the difference in the world," exclaimed Ivor's mother.

"Well, you should have thought of that before," Ivor's father snapped back. "I warned you over and over again. We spent a lot on that vacation, more than even I thought we'd spend. And May won't be able to help us."

"Why not?" cried Ivor's mother.

"She's going to need a full-time, live-in housekeeper to take care of her, and they don't come cheap," his father explained. "And she might live for years. Anyhow, I don't think she'd be too impressed if I asked her for money right now, even for Ivor. Not after our gambling vacation."

Ivor glanced at his reflection in the mirror over the sideboard. He looked strong and sure of himself . . . perfect Kit-cat material. While his parents argued behind him, he checked the paper for tide times. Full tide was in the late afternoon.

The following day, Saturday, he took the bus as usual, delighted with himself for feeling so calm and businesslike. This was what it was like to be grown up and in charge of life. All the same, it gave him a shock to see his great-grandmother so much thinner and frailer than she had looked even six weeks earlier. The flesh of her face draped over its bones, like a theater curtain, ready to drop and reveal the smiling skull below. May's eyes were more deeply sunken than they had been, her hair greasy and uncared for. She looked up nervously as he came into the room, and then, when she saw it was Ivor, beamed with relief and pleasure.

"Ivor, my dear," she said. "What a lovely surprise! I didn't know you were coming."

"I just grabbed the chance," he said. "I've really missed you." He gave her a big bear-hug.

"Tea?" she asked him as Ivor glanced casually at his watch.

"Great!" he said. "But can we go for a walk first? Just to look at everything all over again."

"You go on your own," she said a little sadly. "You'll be freer without me."

"What? Go down the jetty without you?" cried Ivor. "No way!"

"I don't know how good this chair is on a rough road . . ." May sounded doubtful. "I have trouble using the brake, what with my arthritis. But why not?" she added bravely. "Nothing ventured! Nothing gained!"

"I'm strong," Ivor said, beaming. "And the wheelchair's got a seatbelt. I'll fasten you in."

The first part was easy, slightly downhill all the way along a nicely graded main road. But then they turned onto the jetty road, with its potholes and corrugations, and the wheelchair grew harder to manage easily. May cried out in protest, half laughing and half alarmed.

"Oh, heavens, do be careful!"

"Don't worry," promised Ivor, leaning forward to touch the back of her neck as she had often touched his. "I'm going to take *very* good care of you."

"Bless you!" she said. She could not see the expression on his face as he spoke.

Having looked up the tide tables in the paper, Ivor knew exactly when the tide would be high. All the same, it was a relief to him when they came round the corner to see spray splashing up above the sea wall. The water would be deep at the far end of the jetty.

"It *is* lovely to see this view again," May said. "I'm glad you made me come. Now let's go along the jetty, and then hurry back home because I'm beginning to feel rather cold."

"Poor May," said Ivor teasingly. Perhaps he had overdone it, for she suddenly twisted round, trying to look back at him as well as she could.

"Here we go!" he cried heartily, and ran down onto the jetty, pushing her in front of him.

"Stop, Ivor! Stop!" she called breathlessly, but he did not stop. They jolted and swayed along the jetty. *Clonk!* went one particular board under his feet, but there were many loose boards these days. *Twang!* went the tin lid, still lowered over the burned eye. May was silent as her knobbly fingers struggled desperately first with the brake, and then with the catch on the seatbelt. Out beyond the harbor mouth the evening was clear, the sky the color of pure honey. Ivor raced the whole length of the jetty, gathering speed toward the end, even though his lungs were bursting, and then, with a final violent thrust, he sent the wheelchair hurtling down the steps and into the sea. Carried by its own weight and momentum, it toppled straight into the water.

"Oops!" Ivor cried, and actually mimed concern even though he was quite alone. Only now did he truly realize how frightened he had been that May might free herself. If she had bobbed to the surface, he would have had to hold her under, and that would have been horrible. But the chair sank rapidly, taking May with it. He thought he heard her say his name once. Then the water closed over her head and she was gone.

In the end the water grew calm again. The muddy discoloration which had risen to the surface began to dissipate. And at last Ivor felt free . . . free to turn, free to scream as he ran back along the jetty, loose boards drumming urgently under his feet. If his first screams were odd, mechanical cries, by the time his rubber sandals thudded down on the tin lid of the eye, he was screaming in earnest. Real tears were pouring down his face. There was no one to hear, just as there had been no one to see him.

Once on the main road he ran toward the general store, waving desperately at every passing car. The first two drove on, but the third stopped, and he was able to sob out his dreadful tale. His great-grandmother had insisted he take her for a walk, even though he wasn't used to the chair. He had been turning the wheelchair at the end of the jetty, and somehow its front wheels had gone over the top step, and somehow . . . somehow . . .

Ivor wept. It was something he could do quite easily. He wept at intervals for the rest of the evening while people told him it was not his fault, that it had been a terrible accident. As Ivor repeated his story over and over again, he began to believe it himself. It seemed as if it must be true. And then an odd thing happened. As he wept for the last time that evening, his hands across his streaming eyes, he suddenly saw with great clarity a vision no bigger than a bright postage stamp. There was the jetty, dark against the green water. There was its reflection in the sea below, and there, leaning on the railing, was someone holding a bunch of white and yellow flowers. The shock of this sudden picture made Ivor gasp.

"Darling," said his mother. "Poor boy!" He took his hands from his face and looked at her out of swollen eyes. "What a nightmare!" she went on. "But listen, Ivor, I know it seems a callous thing to say, but it wouldn't have been much fun for her from now on. It would have been downhill all the way. It's for the best . . . really, it's for the best." And then she gave him the look of someone sharing a terrible secret, which was almost as alarming as the vision of the figure with the flowers.

After the funeral, Ivor and his parents, along with a few close friends, took a short memorial walk down the jetty. Ivor's father had a fancy to throw flowers into the sea at the spot where May had so often stood gazing up at the sky or out to the mouth of the harbor.

"*You* carry them, Ivor," said his father. "She'd like *you* to be the one to throw them into the sea for her."

Ivor could not refuse. He took the flowers, hiding his horror. They were not from a florist. This bouquet had been gathered from May's own garden—yellow and white daisies mixed with yellow and white roses. Walking down the jetty behind his father, his palms pressed against the stems, Ivor felt those stems changing. Suddenly they felt exactly like May's knobbly fingers. They shifted against his palm, then curled around his own hand and gave it a gentle squeeze.

"Now!" said his father, and Ivor threw the flowers into the water at the exact spot where the wheelchair had sunk four days earlier, shuddering as he did so. The flowers bobbed gently on the slow green ripples.

I-vor! I-vor! I-vor! said the loose boards in rattling voices as sober black shoes walked over them. Though Ivor edged as far away as possible from the tin patch, he knew the eye beneath it was watching him.

"She loved this old jetty," his father said.

"Yes," Ivor's mother agreed, "and you know, it is quite beautiful here. Wouldn't she love to think of us using the house for weekends?"

"Oh, no! It'll be too sad without May," said Ivor quickly. Several friends glanced at him approvingly.

It was a great relief when it was all over and they were back in the city again.

"Well, at least you will be able to go to St. Kit's," said his father. "If you're sure you want to, that is."

"I am sure," said Ivor, surprised at his own calm voice. "I want it more than anything."

In due course he went to St. Christopher's, and though he did not forget the harbor and the jetty, or the wheelchair sinking slowly but steadily from sight, it seemed a small price to pay for the life he now had. Both his parents seemed so relieved and happy, and he had the pleasure of being one of the Kit-cats . . . the top cats in town. Occasionally some people looked critically at his school uniform, but these were triumphant moments, for Ivor knew that they were all secretly jealous of him.

But then, one day, as he put his hand on the railing in the sports pavilion, he felt, not the smooth paint, but the familiar cracked and splintering wood of the jetty rail. There was no doubt about it. At the same time, the breeze, blowing across the athletic fields, suddenly filled with the familiar scent of mud and salt, and of seaweed drying, even rotting a little, at an invisible high-tide line. *Clonk!* said a loose board under his foot, and he thought his heart would stop with sheer fright.

And once these illusions had begun, they happened more and more frequently. The corridors at school stretched themselves before him rather as the jetty had once stretched itself, seeming to promise a dark surprise somewhere along the way. Ivor walked steadily on, hoping the illusion would disappear. It did, only to come again the next day . . . and the day after that as well.

At the end of the week, angry and frightened, he decided to take the bus over the hill, one last time. By walking down the jetty on a bright day, he meant to remind himself that it was merely an old wooden jetty, slowly falling to pieces. This might stop its ghostly intrusions into his city life. The jetty belonged to the *sea* side of the hill and must not be allowed to invade his city side as well.

The bus stopped and he got out, walking quickly past May's old house, which now wore a desolate, overgrown air. Down the familiar winding road he walked, and around the corner. A film of water lying across the mud reflected the blue sky and the hills so perfectly it filled him with amazement. It was as if he were seeing two separate worlds, set edge to edge. Yet the reflected world was not a perfect duplicate of the real one. It was a little smudged, as if he were seeing it through a faint haze . . . a faint fog. Quickly! thought Ivor. Down the jetty—for the last time ever, with a bit of luck. Don't hurry! Don't seem scared in any way! After all, there's nothing to be afraid of. It's all in the mind.

As he stepped onto the jetty, he felt a curious shock. The whole world seemed to flick out of existence for a second and then flick back again. Ivor paused as he looked around. Sky, hills, jetty . . . everything was in place. But that haze was not just a haze but a real fog . . . and how it surged to meet him as he took a step toward it! Where had *that* come from so quickly? Within a moment it was all around him.

But Ivor had walked along the jetty on other foggy days. He knew he could not possibly get lost. *Clonk!* sang the loose board under his foot, then it sighed a little as he stepped off it again. Other loose boards began rattling a chant of *I-vor! I-vor! I-vor!* The fog was so thick by now that it was no longer possible to see ahead, so he watched his moving feet. Suddenly there was the burned eye watching him go by. Someone had pried the tin lid away. Funny, thought Ivor, pausing. He frowned. Hadn't the tide been out? Yet the sea was definitely surging on the other side of that blackened hole. And listen! There! And there again! He could hear the chuckle and slap of waves against the jetty piles.

The fog shifted and parted a little. The tide was indeed fully in, rippling closely under the deck of the jetty. Something bobbed on the ripples . . . a bunch of white and yellow flowers . . . daisies and roses as fresh as the day he had thrown them into the water all those months ago.

Suddenly Ivor knew he could go no farther. He would just have to put up with the ghosts on the other side of the hill. And if he were calm and brave he would probably grow out of them. Anything—*anything*—was better than this. Turning, he began to walk briskly through the fog, back down the jetty again.

Clonk! sang a board under his foot. He stopped short. It had sounded too soon. It had sounded . . . Ivor shook his head as if he were flicking something unpleasant out of his ears and walked on. And there was the eye, watching him retreat. *I-vor! I-vor! I-vor!* said the rattling chorus under his feet. Only a few more yards now, and he'd be on land again. It was at this moment Ivor became certain that someone was walking behind him. He couldn't quite say how he knew, for his own footsteps were the only ones he could hear. All the same, he knew the fog was inhabited. Straining his ears to hear the least sound, he scarcely noticed when he passed the burned eye a second and then a third time. But when he saw it for the fourth time, he understood. He had stepped out of the real world and was now walking through another, terrible place.

Back in the real world, he was suddenly sure, the sun was shining on an old jetty. Back in the *real* world, that old jetty was standing up to its ankles in mud and water and the tide was out. But he was doomed to walk endlessly in either direction, for *this* jetty would go on forever into infinite fog. *Clonk!* Yes, of course! He would hear that sound over and over and over again. And there was the eye, watching him go by once more. It would watch him forever. And those white and yellow flowers would always be bobbing along beside him.

Whatever the thing was in the fog behind him, it was definitely moving closer and closer. Ivor strode on, like a true St. Christopher boy, because he *had* to. If he hesitated, even for a second, he would fall. He tried to keep ahead. At last he even tried to run, but his foot caught on an uneven board and he stumbled.

"Oops!" said a voice behind him—a voice as soft as a small

ripple flopping gently on mud. Knobbly fingers stroked the back of his neck, lightly and lovingly, and Ivor knew that this time their soft caress would last forever.

Charles Mungoshi

The Mountain

We started for the bus station at first cockcrow that morning. It was the time of the death of the moon and very dark along the mountain path that would take us through the old village and across the mountain to the bus station beyond. A distance of five miles, uphill most of the way.

The mountain that lay directly in our path was shaped like a question mark. I liked to think of our path as a question, marked by the mountain. It was a dangerous way, Chemai had said, but I said that it was the shortest and quickest if we were to catch the five o'clock bus.

I could see that he did not like it, but he said nothing more, to avoid a quarrel.

We were the same age, although I bossed him because I was in Form Two while he had gone only as far as Standard Two. He had had to stop because his father, who didn't believe in school anyway, said he could not get the money to send Chemai to a boarding school. We had grown up together and had been great friends, but now I tolerated him only for old time's sake and because there was no one within miles who could be friends with me. Someone who had gone to school, I mean. So I let Chemai think we were still great friends, although I found him tedious and I preferred to be alone most of the time, reading or dreaming. It is sad when you have grown up together, but I could not help it. He knew so little and was afraid of so many things and talked and believed so much nonsense and superstition that I could not be his friend without catching his fever.

From home the path ran along the edge of a gully. It was a deep, steep gully, but we knew our way. The gully was black now and in the darkness the path along its rim was whitish. You never know how much you notice things on a path—rocks, protruding roots of trees, holes, and so on—until you walk that path at night. Then your feet grow eyes and you skirt and jump obstacles as easily as if it were broad daylight.

On our right, away into the distance, was brush and short grass and boulders and other smaller gullies and low hills that we could not see clearly. Ahead of us dawn was coming up beyond the mountain but it would be long, almost till sunrise, before the people in the old village saw the light. The mountain cast a deep shadow over the village.

We walked along in silence, but I knew Chemai was afraid all the time and very angry with me. He kept looking warily over his shoulder and stopping now and then to listen and say "What's that?" although there was nothing. The night was perfectly still except for the cocks crowing behind us or way ahead of us in the old village. We barely made any noise in our rubber-soled canvas shoes. It can be irritating when someone you are walking with goes on talking when you don't want to—especially at night. There was nothing to be afraid of, but he behaved as if there were. And then he began to talk about the Spirit of the Mountain.

He was talking of the legendary gold mine (although I didn't believe in it, really) that the Europeans had failed to drill on top of the mountain. The mountain had been the home of the ruling ancestors of this land, and the gold was supposed to be theirs. No stranger could touch it, the people said. We had heard these things when we were children, but Chemai told them as if I were a stranger, as if I knew nothing at all. And to annoy him, because he was annoying me, I said, "Oh, fibs. That's all lies."

He started as if I had said something I would be sorry for. "But there are the holes and shallow pits they dug that prove it."

"Who dug?"

"The Europeans. They wanted to have the gold, but the Spirit would not let them have it."

"They found no gold. That's why they left," I said.

"If you climb the mountain you will see the holes, the iron ropes and iron girders that they abandoned when the Spirit of the Mountain broke them and filled the holes with rocks as soon as they were dug."

"Who told you all this?" I asked. I knew no one ever went on top of the mountain—especially on that part of it where these things were supposed to be.

"All the people say so."

"They lie."

"Oh, what's wrong with you? You know it's true, but just because you have been to school you think you know better."

I knew he was angry now. I said, "And don't I, though? All these things are just in your head. You like being afraid and you create all sorts of horrors to make your life exciting."

"Nobody has to listen to you. These things happen whether you say so or not."

"Nothing happens but fear in your head."

"Are you arguing with me?" His voice had gathered fury.

"Remember I grew up here too," I said.

"But you haven't seen the things I have seen on that mountain."

"What have you seen?"

"Don't talk so loud." He lowered his own voice and went on, "Sometimes you hear drums beating up there and cows lowing and the cattle-driving whistles of the herd boys. Sometimes early in the hot morning sun you see rice spread out to dry on the rocks. And you hear women laughing at a washing place on a river but you cannot see them."

"I don't believe it," I said. The darkness seemed to thicken and I could not see the path clearly. "I don't believe it," I said again, and then I thought how funny it would be if the mountain suddenly broke into wild drumbeats now. It was crazy, of course, but for no apparent reason at all I remembered the childhood fear of pointing at a grave lest your hand get cut off.

It was silly, but walking at night is unnerving. I didn't mind it when I was a kid because I always had Father with me then. But when you are alone a bush may appear to move and you must stop to make sure it is only a bush. You are not quite sure of where you are at night. You see too many things and all of them are dark. You don't know what these things are, for they have no voice. They will neither move nor talk, and so you are afraid. It is then you want someone older, like Father, to take care of things for you. There are many things that must be left unsaid at night, but Chemai kept on talking of them. Of course the teachers said this was all nonsense. I wished it were so easy to say so here as at school or in your heart as in your mouth. But it would not help to show Chemai that I was frightened too. However, I had to shut him up.

"Can't you ever stop your yapping?"

We had crossed a sort of low hill and were dropping slightly, but very soon we were climbing sharply toward the mountain. It loomed dark ahead of us like a sleeping animal. We could see only its jagged outline against the softening eastern sky. Chemai was walking so lightly that I constantly looked back to see if he was there. We walked in silence for some time, but as I kept looking back to see whether he was there I asked him about the road that I had heard was going to be constructed across the mountain.

"They tried but they could not make it," he said.

"Why couldn't they?"

"Their instruments wouldn't work on the mountain."

"But I heard that the mountain was too steep and there were too many sharp, short turns."

"No. Their instruments filled up with water."

"But they are going to build it," I said. "They are going to make that road and then the drums are going to stop beating." He kept quiet and I went on talking. It was maddening. Now that I wanted to talk he kept quiet. I said, "As soon as they set straight what's bothering them they are going to make that road." I waited for him to answer, but he didn't. I looked over my shoulder. Satisfied, I continued. "And think how nice and simple it's going to be when the road is made. A bus will be able to get to us in the village. Nobody will have to carry things on their heads to the station anymore. There will be a general store and a butcher shop, and everybody will get tea and sugar, and your drums won't bother anyone. They shall be silenced forever."

Just as listening to someone talking can be trying, so talking to someone who, for all you know, may not be listening, can be tiring. I shut up angrily.

We left the bush and short grass and were now passing under a canopy of tall, dark trees. We were on a stretch of level ground. We couldn't see the path here because there were so many dead leaves all over the ground and no broken grass to mark the way.

I couldn't say why, but my tongue grew heavy in my mouth and there was a lightness in my head and a tingling in my belly. I could hear Chemai breathing lightly, with that lightness that is a great effort to suppress a scream; almost a catching of the breath as when you have just entered a room and you don't want anyone in the room to know that you are there.

Suddenly, through the dark trees a warm wind hit us in the face, as if someone had breathed on us. My belly tightened, but I did not stop. I heard Chemai hold his breath and gasp, "We have just passed a witch." I wanted to scream at him to stop it, but I had not the voice. Then we came out of the trees and were in the brush and short grass, climbing again. I released my breath slowly. It was much lighter here, and cooler.

Much later, I said, "That was a bad place."

Chemai said, "That's where my father met witches eating human bones, riding on their husbands."

"Oh, you and your . . ." He had suddenly grabbed me by the arm. He said nothing. Instinctively I looked behind us.

There was a black goat following us.

I don't know why I laughed. Then after I had laughed I felt sick. I expected the sky to come shattering itself round my ears, but nothing happened except that I felt Chemai's fear-agitated hand on my shoulder.

"Why shouldn't I laugh?" I asked. "I'm not afraid of a goat."

Chemai held me tighter. He was shaking as if he had Parkinson's disease. I grew sicker. But I did not fall down. We pushed on, climbing now, not steeply, but enough to make us sweat, toward the old village, into the shadow of the mountain whose outline had now become sharper. It was lighter than when we had started, probably third cockcrow, but it was still dark enough to make us sweat with fear.

"You have insulted her," Chemai said accusingly.

I said nothing. It was no use pretending I didn't know what I was doing. I knew these goats. Lost spirits. Because I had laughed at it, it would follow me wherever I went. It would eat with me, bathe with me, sleep with me. It would behave in every way as if I were its friend or, better still, its husband. It was a goat in body but a human being in spirit. As children, we had seen these goats grazing peacefully on the hills, and there was nothing in them to tell they were wandering spirits. It wasn't until someone laughed at them or said something nasty to them that they would follow in a most ungoatlike manner after whoever had insulted them. And then when this happened it took the elders and much medicine-brewing to appease them, to make them go away.

We walked on very quietly now. We came into the open near the old village school. The path would pass below the old church, and a mile or less further on we would enter the village.

There would be no question of our proceeding beyond the village this morning while it was still dark. I didn't care whether we caught the five o'clock bus or not. I just did not have the strength to cross the mountain before the sun came up.

Also I had to see my grandmother about our companion.

"Let's wait for daylight in the village," I told Chemai. I saw his head bob vigorously in the dark.

My grandmother lived in the old village. She had refused to accompany us and many other people of the village when we moved further west to be near water. She had said this was home— our home—and she would die here and be buried here and anyone who died in the family would be brought back to the old village to be buried. She had had a long argument with my father, but she had been firm.

I did not like the old village nor Grandmother Jape because both of them reminded me of my childhood and the many nightmares in which I dreamed of nothing but the mountain having moved and buried us under it. And then I would scream out and wake up, and the first thing I would smell was Grandmother Jape's smoke-dyed, lice-infested blankets that were coarse and warmly itchy and very uncomfortable to sleep in.

I rarely paid her any visits now, and I wouldn't have stopped to say hello were it not for the goat and my fear of crossing the mountain in the dark. She would know what to do.

We were now below the church.

Suddenly the church gave me an idea. It had two doors opposite each other. We would try to leave the goat in the church. It was a further insult to the goat, but I felt the risk was worth taking.

When I told Chemai he said he did not like it.

"I shall try it anyway," I said.

"She will not stay. She will get out."

We went up the path leading to the church door. We went in. The goat followed. I shouted, "To the other door, quick!"

Chemai rushed for the opposite door. The goat followed him but stopped suddenly when the door banged in its face. I slipped through this other door and shut that one behind me too.

Free. We ran for the village a mile up the hill.

Grandmother's hut was near the center of the village. I knew my way about and in a short time we were knocking on her door, looking back over our shoulders to see whether the goat had escaped. I had to say "It's me, Nharo" before Grandmother would open for us. "Many things walk the night with evil in their hearts," she had once told me.

"What brings you here in the middle of the night?"

"Nothing. We are going to the bus. We want to go to Umtali."

"To the bus at this hour? Are you mad? You must be." She was looking behind us, and I knew our friend had escaped. Quickly we slipped through the door, but the goat followed us into the hut.

Without saying anything Grandmother was already busy with her medicine pots. And suddenly, safe and warm, I felt that the goat was harmless. It was just a wronged friend and would go away when paid. I looked at it. It was a small she-goat, spotless black. In the dim fireglow of Grandmother's hut it looked almost sad.

Grandmother was eating medicines and Chemai was watching her intently. I felt safe. Somebody who knew was taking care of things at last. It is a comforting feeling to have someone who knows take care of those things you don't know.

Susan Cooper

Ghost Story

I'm writing this in longhand, on paper, in my notebook. It's the only way to be private, you know? A computer is no place for secrets—especially my computer. And boy, does this story have to be kept secret, unless I want to be locked up as a crazy person.

You'll see why.

My name's Toby. Toby Waller. I don't have any brothers or sisters, but I have two hyperactive parents, Paul and Ethel Waller. I also have a hyperactive puppy called Seven, which is short for Heinz Fifty-Seven Varieties; we got him from the pound and he's a weird-looking mixture, but cheerful.

My dad's a lawyer. He practices family law, which he says means trying to keep people together, though it seems to me he mostly helps them get divorced.

My mom's a psychotherapist, meaning someone who talks to mixed-up people to help them straighten themselves out. A lot of her clients seem to get divorced too. Don't get me wrong, this isn't a story about divorce, though when I was little I used to worry about my mom and dad because they shout at each other so much. Maybe that's because they both grew up in New York City, which is a shouting kind of place.

I grew up in New York too, till last year. We had this really cool apartment on the East Side, and I could walk to school and play softball in the park, and when there were parades on Fifth Avenue you could hear the music of the bands bouncing along in the distance. Outside my bedroom window I had the branches of a maple tree, different colors all year round. I don't know what got into my parents, to make them want to move.

"There are *trees* in Connecticut," said my mother. "Fields. Rivers. Golf courses."

I said, "We have trees here."

"There'll be less pollution," my father said. "Less violence. A better learning environment."

My father's basically a good person; the trouble is, he feels that he knows everything about everything, and that he's always right. Once I even heard him arguing with the plumber about what kind of washer to put on our kitchen faucet.

I said, "I don't want to leave my friends."

"What friends?" said my father. "I've never seen one, except that kid with the ring in his ear. In Connecticut you'll have dozens of friends."

"*I don't want to move!*"

"That's enough, Toby. You're being childish."

So they sold our city apartment, and they bought a big house with two acres of lawn, in a place called Shady Hollow, Connecticut, where there's nothing but other big houses with two acres of lawn. The house has a pool and a tennis court and next to them a big wooden barn, though if you ask me my parents only call it a barn to pretend that they're living in the country instead of the suburbs.

I hated it. My new school was full of jocks and princesses, all boring. In no time at all my mom and dad had their own friends who came and played tennis on weekends, and I'd hear their hearty outdoor laughter as I sat up in my room at my computer, writing a long journal-letter to my friend Rick, the one with the earring.

And then it started. The haunting.

I started the computer up one morning and scrolled it up

the screen to the place where I'd stopped the day before. I'd written, "My dad still can't bear to lose. He's even worse here than he was in the city. He has to beat everyone at tennis, swim more laps than Mom or me, even race me down to breakfast. It's sick sick sicko." And that's where I'd stopped.

But on the screen there was more.

"Sick sick sick sick SICK. Do it back to him do it back back back. Beat him beat him beat him BEAT HIM BEAT HIM."

That was all. Just two lines. But where had it come from? I didn't write that. Nobody but me had been near this computer since I last wrote in it, and there's no modem to let stuff in from outside. And computers don't invent words themselves—not yet. *Where had it come from?* I sat there staring at the screen, baffled— and worried too, because there was a viciousness behind those words that I didn't think I'd ever felt about my dad. And as I stared, two more words appeared on the screen, underneath the rest, all on their own on a new line.

"KILL HIM."

I jumped up, scared. It was as if the computer were alive. I switched it off, quicker than you're supposed to, and I ran downstairs and grabbed my bike, and went out riding through Shady Hollow, along the peaceful pretty streets all decked out with white and pink dogwood trees. Seven came lolloping along with me. He's old enough to be good at that; he keeps close to the edge inside the bike and doesn't bark at cars. When we reached the golf course I took him for a run, and that took my mind off the computer, so I felt calmer when I came home.

Seven went into the kitchen for a drink of water. It was late afternoon, a lovely spring day, with the sun still slanting down through the trees. I could hear voices and laughter from the porch, so I knew the grownups must have finished their tennis game and be sitting out there having a drink. My father was laughing really loudly, so he must have won. He's a good strong tennis player, really into competitions and tournaments, most of which he wins, and he's always trying to get me involved. I'm big for my age and pretty well coordinated, and he can't understand why I don't want to be like him, and train to be a terrific fierce tennis player and *win*.

I kept away from the porch. Seven came prancing out with an old tennis ball in his mouth, so I threw it for him, to and fro over the lawn, down toward the pool and the tennis court. On the last throw, the ball fell into the pool, and Seven jumped in and swam after it, holding his chin up and puffing. He scrambled out all wet and skinny with the ball in his mouth, shook himself, dropped the ball, and barked at me hopefully. Then suddenly he froze.

He was on the side of the pool nearest the tennis court, which has a wire fence round it to keep balls from bouncing out. He stood there staring at the court. His ears went back and his tail stopped waving, and he began to growl softly, a long, low, threatening sound I'd never ever heard him make before. It was bloodcurdling.

"Seven! Stop it! What's wrong?" I went to him and tried to rub his head, but he took no notice; it was as if he didn't know I was there. The horrible low growling went on, at the back of his throat, but at the same time he must have been scared, because he cringed down toward the ground and began backing slowly away. Then he gave one short, high bark and turned and ran for the house. It was truly weird.

I went through the gate in the fence and on to the tennis court, and peered into the bushes on the other side in case there was a raccoon hiding, or another dog—not that Seven was afraid of raccoons or dogs or anything else. Not usually.

There was nothing there, no sign of any living creature—only a crumpled white towel, a few yellow balls, and a couple of racquets leaning against the fence. Some of my father's friends aren't as passionately careful about their equipment as he is.

I do know all the rules of tennis, and how to serve, and hit overheads and drop shots and lobs and all the rest. You can hardly escape it in our family. My father had me take private lessons two years ago, and there's a tennis team for my age group at this new school—though I was determined to keep away from it, and from all these suburban whizz kids who'd been playing on the family court since they were four years old. I walked back across the court now and picked up one of the racquets and a couple of balls. Nobody was looking, so I went to the baseline and served a ball, just to see if I still remembered how. It wasn't a bad serve, but it hit the edge of the net. I served the second ball, and it went over the net quite fast and bounced in the service court, so I was pleased with myself.

And then the ball came back at me.

I was so surprised I didn't make any effort to hit it. I stood there gaping, and the ball hit the ground to one side of me, well inside the line, and bounced gently away. I looked at it. I looked at the empty court across the net. I thought: *Some serve, Toby!* I must have hit it so hard that it hit the back fence, after its first bounce, and came back at me from there.

I knew as I thought this that it wasn't really possible, but I didn't know what else to think. Would you?

I picked up the ball, and for a long time I held it in one hand and the racquet in the other. There was no sound anywhere except a bluejay squawking in a tree across the yard. Then I took a deep breath and I served. I took care not to hit as hard as I had before;

it was a gentle serve, and there was no way the ball could have hit the back fence hard enough to bounce off.

I saw it go over the net and hit the ground—and then I saw it coming back at me, high and slow, in a long, lazy lob.

I suppose my few tennis lessons had given me enough instinct for the game that I didn't stop to be amazed this time—I just did what you're supposed to do to a lob, which is to run to where the ball's coming down and smash it back across the net with an overhead so hard and fast that it's unreturnable. And I reached it, and wound my racquet backward and I *hit*—

And the ball came back at me, low and swift to the cross court, so fast that I could only stand there helpless, watching as it bounced from the ground to the fence and then trickled gently into stillness.

I stood there, looking at it.

"Hi, Toby! You gonna take up tennis? I thought your dad said you were a lost cause!"

It was one of Dad's tennis partners, Mr. Patterson from next door, a big, easygoing bald man who'd played football for Dartmouth a hundred years ago. I liked him; he talked to kids as if they were people. He came onto the court and picked up the towel and a racquet. I thrust the other racquet at him hastily.

"I was just hitting a few balls. I'll get them for you."

I ran to pick up the balls behind me and then the one lying on the other side of the court. I hesitated before I picked it up, and looked nervously round, but there was nothing, nobody to be seen.

Maybe it hadn't happened. Maybe I'd imagined it. Fat chance.

Mr. Patterson grinned at me as I handed him the balls. "You let me know if you ever want someone to hit them back. I'm not so high-powered as your father."

"Thanks," I said. He was a nice guy; he knew about Dad, and pressure, and winning. "Thanks, Mr. Patterson, but I'm not really into tennis."

I was, though, already. In spite of myself.

Before I went to bed that night I switched on my computer and opened, very nervously, the file holding my letter to Rick. There it was, just as I'd left it when I stopped writing. "He has to beat everyone at tennis, swim more laps than Mom or me, even race me down to breakfast. It's sick sick sicko." But that was all. The extra lines, the mystery lines, weren't there anymore. Instead there was just one word.

"Sorry."

I blinked at it, and I heard myself say in a sort of husky whisper, "That's okay." I guess it was the moment when I first let myself believe I was talking to a ghost.

I switched off the computer, but just before the power died, one more line appeared on the screen, just for an instant, just long enough for me to read it.

It said, "Good overhead. Angle it next time."

Then the screen went blank.

Early the next morning, before school, after my parents had driven off to the station for their commuter train to New York, I went down to the tennis court. I shut Seven in the kitchen, even though it hurt his feelings. With me I took a can of balls and my tennis racquet, which had been lying at the back of my closet for a long time. I hit a ball over the net, and it came back at me, and for half an hour I rallied with my invisible opponent.

After the first shock of accepting the impossible, it was amazing how fast I got used to the idea of playing tennis with someone who wasn't there.

You couldn't call it playing, really; it was practicing. He—I don't know why, but I assumed it was a he—would send me the same shot time after time until I gave it a really good return. Then he'd switch to another kind of shot and do the same, and then come back to the first. Because I couldn't see or hear him, there was the constant challenge of trying to guess where he was, and it fascinated me. I didn't realize at the time that it was the best possible training for anticipating where a real opponent might start heading—so that you could send a ball neatly to a part of the court he or she couldn't reach.

But I didn't know yet that he was training me. I was just having fun.

Every weekday before school I took my racquet to the court, if it wasn't raining, and every day after school until my parents came home from work. Seven couldn't understand it at all; he wouldn't go near the tennis court when I was playing, but would lie mournfully outside the house waiting for me and then jump about trying to lick me all over, as if I'd come back from a long, dangerous journey. Well, perhaps I had.

The only other person around was our part-time housekeeper, Maria, a chubby, smiling lady who loved cooking and polishing, and she couldn't have cared less whether I was hitting tennis balls or roping buffalo, so long as I ate a handful of her chocolate chip cookies when I came in.

The practicing became a part of my life, a real habit. The better I got, the more I enjoyed it. Every so often an encouraging few words would flash through the computer: "Great lob yesterday," or "Try top spin on your ground strokes." The only thing that bothered me on the court was that once in a while, if I made a stupid shot or was too slow getting the hang of something, the ball would come zipping across the net hard and fast and vicious, straight for my head. I always managed to dodge, but it was frightening, like a sign of a mad rage under the surface that might at any moment break out. Always, after it happened, there would be a contrite little "Sorry" on the computer screen that night.

My father had been wrong about my making friends in Connecticut. At school I was a loner, an oddball—the New York kid who read a lot and liked the wrong kind of music. The girls giggled, and the boys left me to myself. So it was only by accident that they found out about the tennis.

Our physics teacher, Mr. Dmitryk, a fiery little dark guy with a big mustache, was at heart an inventor. He loved making machines to demonstrate scientific principles, and he divided our class into three groups, each of which had to take apart some existing machine and make it better. Presumably because Dmitryk was also one of the school tennis coaches, the machine my group was given was one of those gadgets that shoot tennis balls across the net for you to hit back, when you need to practice and haven't got a partner.

With help, the group managed to find out how this thing worked, demolishing it in the process, and then put it back together again. I can't say I was a very useful presence, because math and science are definitely not my thing. I hung about on the edge while they trundled it out to one of the school tennis courts, to show Dmitryk what they'd done, so I was the one sent to do the donkey-work of collecting the balls the thing spewed out.

Dmitryk handed me a tennis racquet. "Never mind if you can't hit them," he said benevolently. "You can just catch them and pitch them back."

I went to the other side of the net, and I looked at the racquet in my hand and I thought: *I won't use this. I'm not one of the*

jocks, I don't want to be one of the jocks. I'll just catch the balls as they come, or fumble for them, and everyone can snigger at the city nerd . . .

But something stopped me. It was as if that racquet were glued to my hand. "Here we go!" someone yelled, and they switched on the machine and the balls started shooting one by one over the net—and one by one I hit them back. Beautifully. I hit them back every which way, top spin forehand, slow spin, slice backhand, deep overhand, high lob; I knew I was showing off, but I couldn't stop.

On the far side of the net everyone was staring at me. They'd forgotten their ball-throwing machine, they were so startled by seeing the New York wimp turned into Tennis Superman. I was pretty startled too; I hadn't realized how much I'd learned. When the supply of balls ran out and I'd hit the last one back with a spectacular top spin forehand down the line, I strolled back to the stunned group, and Mr. Dmitryk came to meet me.

"You never told me you could hit a ball like that," he said.

I said, "Nobody ever asked."

He said, "Can you come to tennis practice tonight?"

So before long I found myself the youngest member of the school tennis team, beating people two or three years older than me. My invisible coach seemed to know this without being told, and he got even more fierce and demanding in the morning practices that were all we had now, the afternoons being taken up by school practice. My parents found out too, of course. Mr. Patterson heard from his daughter, and told them.

My father was furious. "What's the matter with you? I have to hear from my *neighbor* that my son's the star of the tennis team?"

"I'm not a star," I said.

"I'm not allowed to be proud of you?" He was so cross he didn't sound proud at all.

My mother said to me later, reproachfully, "He just wants to feel he can be helpful to you, darling. I mean, you know how fond of tennis he is."

I thought: *You mean, you know how fond of winning he is.* But I didn't say so. I didn't have to. It wasn't ten days before my father, one Saturday when he and my mother had just beaten the Pattersons on our court, called me out of the house to challenge me to a game.

"I'm doing homework, Dad."

He was outside, shouting up to my window. "So do it later. Come on, Toby, take an hour off, for Pete's sake. Three sets. Show me how good you are. You scared I might beat you?"

I sighed and shut down my computer. In the instant before the screen went dark, a line of words flashed across it.

KILL HIM KILL HIM KILL HIM

Then it was gone.

It was the fury again, the viciousness. Shaken, I took my racquet and went out to play my father.

It was a hard match. He won the first set because he was going all out, playing really good tennis. I won the second set because he's thirty years older than me and he'd already played a full game of doubles that morning. In the third set he was fighting back furiously, but so was I; I could feel my invisible coach inside my mind, screaming at me, and my own adrenalin pumping at the same time, pushing me to try to win.

But at the last moment, I caught sight of my dad's face tortured, really *tortured*, with effort, and I knew I must be looking the same—and I suddenly hated it. The whole thing, the competitiveness, the urge to be better than anyone else. I just didn't want to care as much about winning as he did. So I relaxed just enough to take the fierceness out of the ball I was serving, and my father won not only that point but the whole game.

He was delighted, of course. He was out of breath and dripping with sweat, but he ran toward me and actually jumped over the net, as if he were a champion at Wimbledon or something. "Great game, Toby!" he said, and he put his arm over my shoulder. "Keep trying, and you might even be as good as your old man someday."

I looked up and saw my mother wince as she heard him. She waited till he'd gone beaming over to be congratulated by the Pattersons, and then she came and gave me a long hug. She didn't need to say anything; we both knew what he was like.

I didn't dare switch on my computer that evening or for the whole of the next day, because I knew what my ghost would say. He was still furious two days later, and the moment I pressed the switch and the screen grew bright, I saw nothing but a long, angry, unbroken sequence of words: STUPID STUPID STUPID STUPID STUPID . . .

I tried to type "Sorry," but he wouldn't let me in. The same word flowed over the screen, endless, and then the screen went blank, as if my ghost had gone into a sulk and persuaded the computer to do the same. I tried to reach him the next day too, out on the tennis court in the bright early morning, but he was clearly refusing to practice with me and no ball that I hit over the net was returned. They just bounced and lay still.

"Hey, come on!" I shouted into the air. "I need my coach! Don't be mad at me!"

But he was mad, seriously mad. I could feel the anger in the air, prickling all around me like the electricity you can sense in a bad thunderstorm. There was something about his constant seething rage that was far more frightening even than the idea of a ghost itself. For the first time, I began to wonder who he was—or who he had been.

I said to my mother that night, "Who lived in this house before we did?"

"A nice old lady called Ferrold. She moved to Florida. She said she was glad a happy family was moving in." She set the microwave oven time and suddenly looked me in the eye. "*Are you happy here, Toby?*"

"Uh," I said. "Uh—sure I am."

"You look good. Healthy. And you smile more."

"I do?"

"Yes." She gave me a quick hug. "He can't help the way he is, you know. Maybe none of us can."

"I know." I hugged her back, just for a moment, and I thought: *My father? Or my ghost?*

That weekend I went out on my bike and saw Mr. Patterson tinkering with his tractor-lawnmower. He loved mowing his own lawn. He waved to me, and I went over, and because it was him, I said just what was in my head.

"Mr. Patterson? Did anybody really angry ever live in our house?"

His hands stopped moving, and he stared at me with his mouth half open. He said, after a moment, "Why?"

"I . . . just wondered."

Mr. Patterson leaned against the tractor and resettled his baseball cap on his bald head. The eyes in that cheerful face were direct and serious, fixed on me.

"Well," he said. "Well—it's not a pretty story, but maybe you need to know."

I said, "Yes, please."

Mr. Patterson said, "It was about forty years ago, when I was a kid. The family in your house had a boy older than you, about sixteen I guess, and a girl much younger, and the mother was a quiet, gentle soul. But the father was a horror: a cold, hard man with a vicious temper. He'd been in the Marines in World War Two and I think his mind was still stuck there. He ran that house like a military jail: the kids, the mother, they all had to come when he whistled, and if they crossed him, he was terrible. A violent man."

He paused, looking into the past, and shook his head. "The boy was gentle, like his mother, but he had his father's temper. One night they had a terrible row—the father had been drinking, I think, and he'd got mad at the little girl and hit her in the face. The boy went into a terrible rage—I guess he wanted to kill his father—and he grabbed his little sister and ran out of the house with her, furious, and drove off like a maniac in his father's car. And he hit a tree, and he and the little girl were both killed."

I flinched, as if he'd hit me. Like a long noise at the back of my mind I could feel my ghost's pain, and fear, and the endless unresolved rage.

"The father disappeared the next day," Mr. Patterson said. "Just went away. Nobody ever found out what happened to him. Poor Mrs. Ferrold—she stayed on in the house, but she was like a shadow of a person."

I said, "Did the boy play tennis?"

"They built that court for him," Mr. Patterson said. "He was on his way to being junior national champion. His father used to drive him as if he were flogging a racehorse."

"What was the boy's name?"

"Jimmy," Mr. Patterson said.

Our tennis team won the regional championship, and I won the singles for my age group. Then it was summer vacation. My father wanted me to go to tennis camp and couldn't understand why I didn't want to leave home. He also couldn't understand why I wouldn't practice with him, why I went off to play with kids on the school courts instead. I couldn't explain to him that whenever he and I set foot together on our own court, the great wave of rage I felt flooding out from my ghost was intolerable. I couldn't bear it; I felt it would drive me mad. And rage was the only thing I sensed these days; there was no more coaching. It was as if the tennis game that I'd lost, that my father had won, had fixed Jimmy forever in the terrible, angry resentment that had killed him.

Then my father and Mr. Patterson did something I couldn't escape. They organized a neighborhood tennis tournament, to be played on our court. There were no age or sex barriers; everyone played everyone else. And because I had to play to win, for fear of sending my invisible coach over who knew what edge of insane fury, I found myself, at the end, matched in the singles final against my father.

We stood there on either side of the net, facing each other, with dozens of people lined up on chairs outside the fence, watching. I could see my mother, looking very unhappy. My father grinned at me and spat on his hands. "Okay, kid," he called. "Let's see what you're made of!"

It was a long, fierce, terrifying game—terrifying because of my dad's passionate, urgent longing to beat his son, which was embarrassingly obvious to everyone, and because of the great wave of rage against him filling the whole court, which nobody could sense but me. We both played amazingly well. All the time I could feel Jimmy pushing me on, fiercely urging me to win. My father won the first set, I won the second; he won the third, I won the fourth. He was breathing heavily by now, getting tired. Then we were five games to four in the last set, and it was my serve.

I sent a fast serve zooming down the line, and my father dived but couldn't reach it. Fifteen-love. I served again, and he drove it hard but hit the net. Thirty-love. I could see that tortured look on his face again, the anguished desire not to lose. But I didn't care. Jimmy was inside my head, shrieking KILLHIMHILLHIMKILLHIM, and all I wanted was to win. I served two unreturnable aces in a row, and the second had my father skidding face-down over the court as he missed it—and I'd won the match.

I didn't hear the applause. The rage roaring through my mind had become a great vindictive shriek of delight as my ghost waited, gloating, for my defeated father to raise an embittered, furious, beaten face. Waited for triumph, with all the built-up rage of forty resentful dead years.

But it didn't happen. Instead, my dad scrambled to his feet, threw down his racquet, ran at the net and jumped over it, just as he had when he'd beaten me. He flung his arms round me in a huge hug and then pushed me back, holding my shoulders with his hands, looking at me with an enormous, delighted grin like a little kid faced with the Christmas tree. It occurred to me for an instant that he really was a little kid, much littler than me, somewhere in his head. The delight was absolutely genuine. He said joyfully, "Toby, you're a marvel! *I'm so proud of you!*"

Then he hugged me again and kissed me on the cheek, and I couldn't say a word. On the other side of the fence I could see my mom, beaming.

And gradually I felt all the rage and resentment and hate drain away out of the air around that tennis court and that house, and instead there was a wonderful, happy astonishment everywhere, and peacefulness, and a small breeze rustling the maple trees against the blue sky.

I switched on the computer before I went to bed that night. I typed in: *It's all right now, Jimmy. It's all right. Sleep well.*

And just for a moment, there were more words on the screen.

I will. Good night, Toby. Play well. Good-bye.

Then the screen went dark, and he was gone.

Roberto Piumini

Don't Read This!

Those who read this, take care.

I am not just an ordinary story. You would do well not to read any further. I am dangerous. Even worse: I am fatal.

Are you going to read on all the same?

Do not be curious, my friend: not this time.

In reality, I am not a story: I am a curse. And the reason why, that is something no one is allowed to know and is none of your business. Perhaps I have been written by the Devil.

So I am warning you: Do not read this. Do not read me. Reading me brings bad luck.

Why are you still reading? Imagine you have walked into a street and someone shouts at you from the distance, "Stop! Come back! That's a terrible street, a dangerous street, a deadly street! Further on, there are ravines, wild animals, and murderers!" If someone shouted these words at you, would you go on walking then? I do not think so; you would stop and go back.

Why are you reading on, then? You have been told that this story is a curse: it brings bad luck. Stop here, do not read another line. Read another story; there are so many in the world, even in this book.

But no, you are still reading. Perhaps you do not believe me, you want to know why I am cursed. The fact of the matter is, reckless friend, that everything written in this book happens while it is being read. Not only "in the story" or "in your imagination," no, it really happens, in reality, in this world.

I am a terrible magic spell.

Forget it, friend; go and read something else.

Are you still reading? Have you not been warned enough? You feel safe, you think: "Nonsense! What on earth can happen if I read it? Who sees me? Who knows?"

Okay, have it your way. You will learn the hard way. Remember, what you read here will happen at precisely the same moment as you read it. It happens *because* you read it.

If you do not want it to happen, do not read. Stop now, at this line.

You have not stopped. Then stop at least as soon as you read something nasty, something unpleasant. If you stop, the event will stop too. If you stop reading before "it" happens, it will not happen. I cannot stop and warn you again; once a story has started, it has to go on until it ends. But you can stop at any time. You are free to discontinue reading. Stop, before terrible things happen.

Well then, Milovic held his machine gun firmly and crouched even lower against the damp tree trunk. He could feel the cold of the thick layer of snow through the soaked material of his trousers; it all but caused pain in his knees. "Waterproof uniforms," they had claimed at Supplies. Idiots. They sat back there outside the battle zone distributing weapons and ammunition, unloading trucks. They did not have to stand still for hours in the cold, crouched in uncomfortable positions without even being able to move their heads. Those accursed Bosnians could not shoot, that is true, but if a bullet hits you, even when it has been shot badly, then you've had it.

But now there was no more shooting from the house. Not for at least twenty minutes. Or for perhaps as long as half an hour? You could hear the gunshots down there, near the Ravezia woods, close to the bridge. Faint gunshots, like the notes of a hymn in the far distance, over and over again, almost soft in the pale white air. Almost pleasant to listen to. They made you sleepy. Furious, Milovic shook his head. That was all he needed, that he should fall asleep now. First he had to drive those Bosnian rats out of their hole. They would not give themselves up. All the better: if the others do not give themselves up, it is more of a war. Things are clearer, more definite.

He lifted his head half an inch, then another half an inch. He looked. The house, with its dirty walls and the bullet holes round the window, stood motionless in the cold. It looked like a painting. Too still.

Hit, they had not been hit. Perhaps they had left . . . But Van was on the other side, watching the back. You would have heard the shots. No, they were still inside there, those two. Or that one. Perhaps there was only one who shot round indiscriminately to make it appear that he was not alone. And in that way he wasted ammunition, the idiot.

Almost oppressed by the total silence of the house, Milovic lifted his head a little higher. Perhaps he had used all his ammunition, that Moslem swine.

He decided to move forward a little. He aimed his machine gun and loosed a volley without aiming at anything in particular, so as to frighten them. Then he started off on a short sprint, bending forward, up to the trunk of a huge birch—fifteen paces from the house. He felt a cold shiver running down his spine. He knew what it was. The fear that hit him immediately and mercilessly. He pressed himself closer against the tree trunk; his breath formed two or three clouds of steam in the cold air.

There was no shooting from the house.

Suddenly he became angry.

"Van!", he shouted impatiently into the air. He wanted to

know if his mate was still there on the other side. Van was a strange character, no coward, but odd. He was capable of walking off in the middle of a battle to ask for a cigarette from someone in the trucks half a mile further on. He could fall asleep in the snow, in the middle of gunfire.

"Van! Are you there?"

Silence. In the house and in the wood. Here and there he could hear the echo of his voice, like the crack of a whip.

Milovic frowned. He could now feel the cold not only in his knees but in his whole body. He must eat and get warm. He wanted to build a fire.

He decided to take the plunge. They did not call him "Milovic the war-horse" for nothing. It would not be the first time that he had attacked a Bosnian in hiding. He knew what he had to do. He leaned to one side and looked. The house was motionless and quiet. Those two would have only a few bullets left, if any at all. Who knows who had trained them: possibly some Bedouin or other from Iran. They send people who fight in the desert to train people who have to fight in the mountains. Idiots, they deserve to die as idiots.

He jumped up, fired in the direction of the window and the door, and went up to the wall of the house. Then there were the muffled echoes from the gunshots, short from nearby and long from a distance and then nothing. Even at the end of the valley, there were no more shots to be heard.

He stood with his back against the cold stones and thought, "I'll count to ten and then I'm going in." No one in his group was braver than he. But he counted to seven and impatiently he went for it. With his legs wide apart, he stood in front of the door and shot resolutely. Splinters flew everywhere. He kicked under the lock and then he kicked the door down.

Cursing Allah, Milovic went inside, shooting in a semicircle around him. He riddled walls and the remains of farm furniture; he smashed into smithereens the glass in a large photograph of a bridal couple, arm in arm on the Mostar bridge.

This time he cursed his own God and stood still. A window was open opposite the door. He looked outside and saw hasty footprints in the snow. He cursed again under his breath. Who knew how long they had been gone while he had been standing back there with his knees freezing in the snow. And Van? It would be better if he were dead. Van brought bad luck. One of these days he would put a bullet in Van's body during an attack. It would have been better if Van had fought with the Bosnians from the beginning, then they would have lost by now.

He looked round the room and saw the chimney. Small and black. A chimney meant fire. And there lay firewood, not dry branches exactly but firewood.

Milovic kicked the riddled door, breaking it down still further, gathered up a heap of rotting wood, made a pile of it in the hearth, rolled up the photograph, put it underneath, and lit the fire. A black smoke, strange and biting, began to rise. The door burned with difficulty, the flames licking here and there like the tongue of a snake in hiding.

Milovic coughed, then stiffened. He had heard someone else coughing too. He took his machine gun and held it firmly, and turning his head to the left, he listened.

He heard that coughing again, quick, thin, restrained. It came from under the floor. He could see the trapdoor, right under the table. Softly, he lay down on his knees and placed his ear against the wooden floor that was dark and greasy and smelled of leather and food which had been prepared there for a hundred years. He could hear the whispering of a woman who was begging someone to be quiet. Then another fit of coughing but smothered by something made of cloth.

A woman and a child, of course. And who else? Maybe that swine of a Bosnian with one last bullet in his barrel.

The wood from the door was burning well now. The smoke hung high in the room against the beams. Below, the hearth spread a pleasant warmth.

There were two possibilities. The first, difficult, dangerous, or tedious: move the table, open the trapdoor, look and see who was under it, judge whether it was dangerous or not, and possibly interrogate, guard, escort . . . and that way lose the lovely warmth which had almost dried his knees that had been soaked with snow. Milovic did the second. He stood up slowly and took a hand grenade out of his rucksack. To avoid the trapdoor, he searched with his eyes for a suitable opening. There was one just big enough along the wall, half a yard from the door: a passageway for field mice.

He stepped over the doorstep looking for shelter, pulled out the pin, stretched out his arm, and pushed the hand grenade into the hole: a small, dark war-mouse. He heard a thud on the floor, a woman's cry; suddenly a gust blew through the room and the dark smoke began to twist wildly like a merry-go-round full of black angels. Not even all that much noise.

Then it stopped and remained silent. The fire, which had almost gone out because of the displacement of air, began to crackle in the hearth again.

Milovic went inside, walked along the wall, and crouched by the fire. He stretched his hands out and did not move, at the same time sucking the inside of his lip where he could feel a painful sore.

That was due to the gunk they gave the troops to eat in the

mountains. In Sarajevo, they certainly got better food.

In any event, a fire brings comfort.

You are still reading: it has happened. You are not the one who made it happen, but by reading you have allowed it to happen. That is the curse. It is over. You have done it. You did not stop, you went on reading.

Do you understand now?

Do not read this story any further; stop here. You have read enough. If you do not read, I cease to exist. The things that have been written in me will not happen. They will not exist in the world.

Why are you still reading? You know: I cannot stop, I am a story. But you are a person. You know: if you read me, the things that you read about will happen.

Perhaps you think that not all the things in me will be terrible. Perhaps you think that there will be beautiful things, nice things. And that you, when you read about them, will let them happen ...

Is it worth taking the risk? Talking of bombs, if you should find a bomb, would you go on playing with it in the hope that it is an imitation bomb, made of chocolate with flowers that pop out when it explodes?

Do not read on further now. Do not wait until the next line. You can do it, stop.

Chavier, captain of the *Godard Super*, brought the ship onto a new course. A rather northerly course, slightly unusual in the Atlantic Ocean, a little too near the icebergs but not so near as to make it abnormal. It was just that it was improbable that they would meet other merchant ships or fishing boats, not at this time of the year.

It was a beautiful day; the sea was as smooth as glass. It did not seem like an ocean at all, more like one of the East European inland seas or the northern area of the Adriatic Sea near Triest, where Chavier had sailed with small tankers for years. But this was very much the ocean: many billions of tons of water, a secret depth with its fish, mysterious whales, and underwater monsters. All silent creatures, creatures that cannot talk.

The door of the wheelhouse opened. Shippers came in and took his pipe out of his mouth. He did that every time; it was a sort of mark of respect for the captain. Then he put it slowly back into his mouth, enjoying it just as a greedy child does with a sweet.

Shippers glanced at the instrument panel and rubbed his chin. Then he looked ahead and said in a calm voice, "So far north, John? That way, the crossing will be at least ten miles longer."

Chavier gave no answer. He concentrated on the instruments as if he wanted to check something and then looked ahead again at the vast, dark green sea. Shippers waited without saying anything. If the captain did not feel like talking, you should not insist on doing so. They were friends, that was obvious, but anyone preferring to remain silent was his own best friend.

After a while, Shippers went downstairs to the deck. It was his last voyage and he wanted to enjoy it. Forty-three years in the merchant navy: enough to make one an "old sea dog." When he returned from this voyage, it would be over. He would see the sea from his house set on the high rocks in Cornwall. Together with Elizabeth, who looked forward to the time they would spend together. And from Taunton, Mary and George would bring Jimmy to visit him much more often. Shippers had a lot of stories to tell them. Just looking at the sea makes the stories come automatically . . .

He walked alongside the hold and stopped to have a chat with Peterson, who was in charge of the engine room and had come up on deck to smoke a cigarette in the fresh air. Twenty years together, on many ships, they knew each other well.

"They loaded up in a strange way in Liverpool, don't you think?" said Peterson, his gaze directed straight to the north, to the cold polar region.

"Strange? I don't know, Paul, I was in the wheelhouse. Chavier assigned me the customs forms. And Scatts kept an eye on the stowing . . . Why do you say 'strange'?"

"I don't know, Charlie . . . The barrels are usually placed in the middle of the hold, aren't they?" said Peterson.

"Certainly, they're more stable there. And they're easier to unload on arrival."

"Exactly."

"How do you mean 'exactly,' Paul?"

"Because this time they've put about a hundred just at the top of the stairs and they haven't even tied them properly, I think . . . If we get into one of those storms near Newfoundland, those things will roll like ten pins at a bowling—"

"But what does Bob say about it?"

"He says that everything's in order, that they're secure enough. I don't know, there's a strange atmosphere hanging in the hold . . . "

"I'll go and have a look," said Shippers.

They were standing near the hatches to the hold when they saw Shippers approaching. They looked at each other, Bob, in charge of the hold, and two of his men, robust Irishmen with pale faces.

"Bob, I'd like to have a look at the cargo," said Shippers calmly.

"Oh, why?" said Bob, with a short jerk of his head that made his sandy-colored hair fall back. "Scatts has checked everything."

"Calm down," said Shippers. "I only need to check the chests from Manchester, Bob. They've made a mistake in the numbering, I have to note down their position in the register. It'll take two minutes."

"Does the captain know about it?" asked Bob, and he scratched at paint peeling off the table he was leaning on. "You know that the hold can be opened at sea only on his orders."

"Call him, Bob, I don't want to waste any time." Shippers' voice now had a hard tone to it, that of the second in command. He could make his voice sound even meaner when he was telling Jimmy stories about pirates as they walked along Cape Hartland.

"I'll open it," said Bob peevishly.

A quarter of an hour later, Shippers went into the wheelhouse again. He did not have his pipe in his mouth or in his hand.

"There's something wrong with the cargo, John," he said in a decisive tone.

"What?"

"Scatts must have gone mad. He's placed about a hundred green barrels with 'Special Solvent' written on them on the edge of the hold, tied with only a bit of thin rope. At the first sizable wave they'll start moving in the hold."

"Scatts knows what he's doing, Charlie," said the captain slowly, without looking at him.

"Not this time, John. There'll be no stopping this cargo even at a mere wind-force two."

"Look how calm the sea is," said the captain with a strange grimace. "There's not a breath of wind to be expected in the next three days."

Shippers was silent for a second as if surprised. He had a

strange, unreal feeling.

"The crossing takes eight days, John," he said then.

The captain heaved a deep sigh, then turned round and faced him.

"Those barrels are lying all right where they are, Charlie," he said.

"What do you mean, 'all right where they are'?"

"I mean we're going to dump them tonight."

"In the sea?"

"Where else?" said the captain, and he looked ahead again.

Shippers put his hand in his pocket nervously. He felt his pipe, but he did not take it out. His face was red and he had a sharp, burning feeling in his stomach. He realized he was the only one who didn't know what was going on.

"What kind of stuff is it, John?" he asked.

"I don't know and I don't care either," answered Chavier, not looking in his direction. "It's stuff that's bad for the world and it has to disappear. Tonight we'll open the side hatch in the hold and push those few barrels overboard. No one will know anything about it."

"And nor would I if I'd been sleeping in my cabin, would I?" said Shippers bitterly. His stomach was burning constantly now, just as it did when he had drunk two beers too many in Henry Sheilley's pub.

"The shipowner has no objections, Charlie," said the captain. "There's money for everyone, for you too. And it's more than a nice tip, Charlie. You could have the roof of your house in Raswill repaired."

Shippers laid his hand on his stomach but without rubbing it.

"It must be deadly stuff, John," he said. "It must be terrible rubbish if they don't want it even in Truro. The sea is fifteen or eighteen thousand feet deep here, you know that. The pressure will break them before they reach the bottom, and the current . . ."

"They told me the barrels were reinforced, Charlie," said the captain as he took off his cap and scratched his head. "They're made of a metal that stays intact up to thirty thousand feet deep."

"Nonsense, John. I've seen them. They're just ordinary storage barrels."

Silence fell. From the depths of the ship, only the low, heavy noise of the engines sounded. Then Shippers said in a strange voice, "Whales come here in the spring with their young ones. My grandson Jimmy explained that to me, he knows all about whales . . ."

Silence again.

"Go to bed, Charlie," the captain said. "Tomorrow morning, everything will be over. The sea is big and won't be put upon, not even by us. And if we don't do it, somebody else will, perhaps those louts from Hamburg, they dump near the coastline . . . Go to bed now. It's your last voyage, don't spoil it. Scatts will be coming up in a minute, and it's better if you . . ."

Shippers interrupted him: "He's the one who's in charge of all this, isn't he?"

Chavier gave no answer.

With searing stabs of pain in his stomach, Shippers left the wheelhouse. To the left of the prow, the sun hung low above the sea now. The ship was following the sun but would never reach it. From behind, from the east, a dark cloud was approaching.

Shippers went down to his cabin to lie down so that the burning feeling would subside. After that, he would go and look for Scatts and . . . Perhaps it would be better to speak to Peterson and the others first. Probably no one in the engine room knew anything about this matter. Perhaps they only knew about it in the hold. Seven or eight men.

He went and stretched out on his stomach on the narrow bed, breathing slowly, knowing what was good for him. Immediately he felt a little better; he had his stomach ulcer fairly well under control. He could cope with it. Suddenly he was overcome by sleep. He dreamed confusedly: Jimmy, the seagulls at the Cape, and then Jimmy sitting astride the mother whale's back as she greeted him from the other side of the rocks. Then Elizabeth running up the path to the lighthouse with a pan of doughnuts in her hands . . .

Perspiring and stupefied, he woke up. He sat up uncertainly. Through the porthole on his right, the dark mass of the ocean had swallowed up the last of the daylight.

He stood up, breathed in deeply, and left his cabin. He began to go down the stairs to the third deck in search of Peterson. It was dark at sea. As never before, he enjoyed the salty air of the Atlantic Ocean.

He was halfway down when four strong arms pulled him mercilessly from the stairs and threw him over the railing. As he flew, he managed to think of Jimmy for a moment and blew him a desperate kiss.

You see, you have done it again. You went on reading and what you read has happened. No, of course not: you did not throw Shippers into the sea and you will not dump those hundred green barrels into the Atlantic Ocean tonight, but it has happened, it is going to happen, because you read it.

Do you want to go on? Really?

I have to: I am the story. But you are not me. Think about that when you read this . . . You are just in time: stop. If you do not read this, they are only things on paper, they do not exist, they are not true. But if you read them, they happen. That is the curse.

Do not read any further than this line.

The first warnings of the weak spots came eleven days ago. And even before he informed the Emergency Commission, the engineer responsible did his duty: he turned the reactor down to half power. Then came the inspector, who compiled the report 7455/RS, which was sent to management immediately. The general manager, engineer Francesco Di Sghinopoli, raised an eyebrow while he was reading it and had engineer Pasquali, head of the Technical Department, brought to him.

"Pasquali, I have read the report. Tell me the facts briefly."

"It's what we already knew, sir," answered Pasquali in the humble tone his voice took when he was speaking to his superiors and which he could not change even if he wanted to.

"What did we know, Pasquali? We knew so many things."

"I meant that we knew about the outside casing of the reactor, sir. In layers three and four, which are indicated in the report as being thirteen and fourteen, there is a stain which indicates third-degree decay. There's always been an unevenness on that spot, but yesterday a clear stain could be seen . . ."

"How big was it, Pasquali?"

"A spot of about ten square inches with a strange shape . . . It looks like a butterfly. Probably—"

"Through all the layers?" interrupted Di Sghinopoli.

"Yes, it looks like it . . . It's difficult to carry out a test in depth at that point when the reactor's warm, you know . . ."

"I know, Pasquali. Who knows about this matter apart from you, the engineer responsible, and the Emergency Commission?"

"As far as I know, nobody else, sir."

"It would be better not to let this leak out. You know how the outside world is waiting to swallow us whole. The press . . ."

"I know, sir. Everyone will remain silent here."

"You'll be hearing from me in the near future, Pasquali."

The butterfly-shaped stain, a problem from the beginning, was due to an unevenness in the steel in tank number three. They had known all along, but the chance that the steel would give way was estimated at 0.003 percent. Much smaller than the chance of an earthquake with a strength of 8 on the Richter scale occurring in the area. Practically nil. And because the tank had already been installed when the weakness was discovered, and replacement, apart from the cost, would have delayed activating the reactors by three months, the commission in authority had given the green light, the only advice being that the metal in the tank should be checked every two months in any event . . .

The butterfly had not moved for three years, as if it did not exist. It listened calmly to the deep electric hum that came through the insulated walls: atoms that broke, split, powerful secret rays of light.

Then the steel, which knew nothing about statistics and calculations of probability, had started crumbling away. But slowly, one atom, two, five, ten each time. Not in a hurry. Atoms, who can count them?

One who was in a hurry was party chairman Spinardi, who had to leave for a party congress. And because he had been informed by the Emergency Commission, he spoke to Di Sghinopoli.

"Sir, as usual, I am relying on you completely . . . but the circumstances. I mean, without forgetting the necessary caution, take into account that the elections are in two weeks and you know what kind of disturbances the anti-atomic energy movement can cause and will continue to cause . . . Any bungling or even a shadow of bungling, a problem in the atomic power station, just now, you understand what that means. In parliament, they'd dance on the tables with joy. And I fear that when the people go to vote, with the scant and biased information they have, they might let themselves be carried away by any exaggerated feelings of worry . . . "

"I quite understand what you mean, sir," said Di Sghinopoli, who was better at deciphering the language of politicians than at deciphering a physics calculation.

Deep down in the steel, the butterfly knew nothing of the election or of opportunism. It moved on slowly, throbbing: a thousand atoms, ten thousand, a million: there are so many atoms, who can count them? It seemed to be still a caterpillar waking up from its winter sleep of a thousand years rather than a butterfly.

In the meantime, another butterfly fluttered out of the mouths and ears of the people, despite the attempts to keep it a secret: the power station has had one of the reactors turned down to half power. The message reached certain people who thought it was important. One of the dreaded newspapers printed the news in a corner of the front page: "It has been confirmed that one of the reactors at the Poffio atomic power station is causing problems. The third reactor has been reduced to half power. If this situation continues for more than three days, it means, as you know, that serious damage to the installation has been detected."

On his return from the party congress, Spinardi rang Di Sghinopoli. His voice was cold.

"You had promised discretion, sir."

"I have done everything possible, *onorevole*. But the power station is large, there are more than four hundred employees. And although it seems incredible, there is of course someone here on the inside who sympathizes with the anti-atomic energy movement . . ."

"The damage has already been done, Di Sghinopoli. We must find a solution."

"What do you propose, *onorevole*?"

"You are the expert, Di Sghinopoli. You're not in this position just because of your scientific capabilities but also because of your, let's say, political skills in settling matters."

"Yes, you see *onorevole*, in this case I don't think—"

"Is it true what they are saying about the three days? I mean what was in the newspapers today?"

"Well, uh, *onorevole* . . . that's the case in practice. A reduction in the capacity for less than three days, called Pause Phase One, is sufficient to carry out normal checks. For longer than three days, Pause Phase Two takes effect, and that means that there are serious abnormalities or defects."

"All right, Di Sghinopoli. But then we're surely talking about a Pause Phase One here, aren't we?"

"But you see . . . to be honest, I think that a third-grade stain of this size demands that— "

"Tell me honestly: is it something dangerous, is there an immediate danger?"

"I . . . an immediate danger, perhaps not. I wouldn't say it was immediate. But there must be a thorough—"

"Under normal circumstances, everything would be different, Di Sghinopoli, but we've got elections hanging over us. Listen, if the reactor were to be turned on again, nothing would happen, would it?"

"Well, it would seem as if everything was under control, but—"

"I haven't finished yet. The elections are in eleven days. We would only have to keep the reactor burning up to election day: about ten days. Then, on election day, you can turn it off and carry out all the checks. Don't you think that'd be a good move. Di Sghinopoli?"

"Yes, a good move, *onorevole*, but I hesitate ..."

"Don't hesitate. You'll be completely covered in making this decision. And I'd prefer not to do it, but in this situation I must remind you that the existence of the power station and also your personal position is largely due to my political influence ... The votes are our energy, Di Sghinopoli; the election reactor must work for us ..."

"I've always been grateful to you, *onorevole* ... It's just that a reactor ... Since ..."

"My dear Di Sghinopoli, just ten days. After that, you can check, overhaul, replace. If the elections go off satisfactorily, which I hope they do, then I promise you that you can do whatever you feel is necessary for the power station. What do you think?"

A silence fell. Di Sghinopoli perspired and thought carefully. There really was a good chance that no problems would arise, at least no immediate problems, if they turned on the reactor. A stain indicating third-degree decay is just a stain indicating third-degree decay. If you keep an eye on the vibrations and if you place a few extra sensors so that you can, if necessary, first ...

"I'm waiting for your answer, Di Sghinopoli," said the member of parliament.

"All right, *onorevole*, tonight we'll have the reactor going at full power again," said Spinardi slowly.

"Sensible decision," remarked the member of parliament.

Eight days later, that is, two days before the election, in other words, today, the butterfly in the steel has awoken and has started to vibrate unexpectedly. Its parts, billions and billions, came to life, instantaneous and fragile. Deep in the metal, it tore. That is where the casing broke—the casing that, together with the other layers, had kept the horrifying strength of the nuclear fission in check. The deadly light flashed outside, forcing its way across the global square. Billions and billions of minute butterflies, a jumble of toxic rays, fluttered in the air.

This story has finished too.

And you are still reading. What has been told has therefore happened. Happens, is going to happen. Perhaps you do not believe it. You smile, thinking that it has been a game, intimidation.

I wish that were so, really.

But please, go to the window if you would. You can go now: the story is finished. This one and every other one. There is nothing more to read or to do.

Whoever reads this, go to the window. In the air above the city, to the north, there hangs a strange, greenish-colored cloud.

It is no thundercloud.

Klaus Kordon

The Ravens

The road twists down the mountain and disappears somewhere in the evening mist that is hanging over the valley. The valley is not marked on Axel's walking map, but shouts rise up from the mist. A woman's voice calls something and another one answers.

There must be a village down there. He need not spend the night in the woods. Axel puts his knapsack on his back once again and walks on. In his imagination he can already see an inn with cozy corners and a kitchen that smells good. He can see himself sitting at a table with a plate full of sausage, cheese, and bread in front of his nose and a glass of cool wine. How he would eat and drink! And after that, fall asleep in a soft, freshly made bed and sleep, sleep, sleep! He has not slept well for days now. Repeatedly he felt the dampness of the woodland soil in his sleeping bag and lay tossing and turning until the first gray of the dawn. But tonight he will sleep!

The road, which is actually a path that appears to be seldom used, is getting steeper and steeper. Axel has to walk more slowly and has to hold on to the trees and bushes so as not to stumble. But finally he reaches the bottom of the valley. The path slopes down no longer. Carefully he gropes his way through the mist. He can hear hoarse cries, scratching and creaking. Evidently, few tourists come to this valley since there are so many kinds of animals living here. The creaking noise comes from the trees, groaning with old age.

Axel stands still to listen. Where did the voices come from? More to the right or more to the left? He hears nothing. The only sound is the creaking of the trees and the screeching and scratching of the birds. If only he knew which way he had to go. Slowly, Axel walks on further. The woodland soil under his feet becomes softer and soggier. He must go back. Otherwise, he might perhaps end up in a swamp. He turns round, walks until the ground becomes firmer, and keeps to the right. A short while later, it is soggy again under his feet. He has to turn round again and this time goes to the left. After a few yards he heaves a sigh of relief. The path becomes firmer. There is a road to the farms in the valley after all.

In the meantime, it has become pitch dark. Axel takes his flashlight out of his knapsack and directs it toward the bushes and in front of him. But he sees nothing. The mist is like a wall. He stands still to listen again, but there is nothing to be heard except the rustling of the wood.

Should he unroll his sleeping bag after all? Who knows how long he still has to walk through the night before he reaches one of the farms. But the bed! He would so love to sleep in a real bed again! Even if there is no inn in this valley, he is sure to be able to find shelter somewhere there . . . Axel decides to try his luck. If within half an hour he has still not found any houses, he will give up searching.

After just three steps, Axel stands still again. He has heard something. It is music. Very soft violin music. Could it be that one of the people in the valley plays the violin? That is a good sign! Walking more quickly, he trips over the root of a tree that is growing right across the path and hurts his foot.

The violin music sounds louder, louder and louder. The violin player is coming toward him! Quickly Axel hides behind the tree with the root that tripped him up. He is not afraid, just careful. A man who walks through the wood and plays the violin at night must be a strange character. The music comes closer and closer. When the violin player is just two or three yards away from him, Axel switches on his flashlight, comes out from behind the tree, and sees his mistake right away. It is not a man but a girl wearing jeans and a sweater. It is not a violin in her hands but a portable radio-cassette-player.

Carefully Axel shines his light into the girl's face. He has not frightened her! She is very calm and even smiles a little.

"Did you call just now?" Axel asks. He tells her that he heard voices and is looking for an inn.

"Call?" the girl repeats without answering the question. "There is no inn here," she says then. "There are only three houses in the valley. But there is sure to be a bed for you."

She walks slowly ahead of Axel and tells him that she is on vacation here and that she is all alone in the valley except for three old women.

"Three old women?" Axel finds it all very peculiar. A young girl on vacation alone in a remote valley? That is almost as strange as his plan to walk right across the Black Forest and to become one with nature.

"I like being alone," the girl says again smiling strangely. Axel cannot see it, of course; he can only sense it. Nevertheless, he is certain the girl is smiling. The girl with the radio must have guessed his thoughts. How else could she have answered as she did?

The girl says that she is staying with her grandmother, an old woman who has never been out of this valley in her life.

"What's this valley called? It's not marked on my map."

"It's Ravens' Valley. It's not marked on any map. People have forgotten it."

"Ravens' Valley? That sounds horrifying," says Axel, laughing.

"Are there that many ravens here?"

"No. Maybe there used to be. At the moment there are still three ravens living in the valley. But sometimes there are four."

How can the girl know that there are sometimes three and sometimes four? Does she count them every day? But Axel does not ask.

"So you think I'll be able to find a bed in Ravens' Valley?" he says.

"Yes, I'm sure," the girl answers. "There's always a bed free in the house next to ours. Of course, it's a very old house. There's no electricity or running water in Ravens' Valley. But someone who wants to get to know nature won't mind that."

As if struck by lightning, Axel stands still. "How do you know that?" he asks the girl. "Who told you that?"

"What?"

"That I want to get to know nature."

"You said that just a moment ago, didn't you, when we met each other."

He is certain that he did not say that. This girl can read his thoughts! Axel begins to get a strange feeling, but the girl smiles and holds out her hand.

"My name's Anne," she says.

"And mine's Axel. But of course you already know that." Axel shakes the girl's hand.

The girl does not respond to his remark, and silently she leads Axel on through the valley.

A witch! thinks Axel as he walks behind the old woman with the smoky candle in her hand up the steep stairs to the attic room. It is true, the old woman has offered him a room just as Anne had promised, but she made a face as if she would rather he left again.

The door to the attic room creaks in its hinges.

"There we are! Here's the bed. And there's the chest with bed linens." With the candle, the old woman lights up the corner where the chest stands, and after that, Axel's face. She looks up at him, smiling, rattles her jaw, and leaves.

Axel switches on his flashlight and lays it on the table. He had dreamed of a glass of wine and a plate of bread, and what did he have now? A strange old woman who is gruff at first and then smiles suddenly as if she is up to something, a dusty attic room, and a terrible hunger. He puts down his knapsack and kneels in front of the chest so that he can get at the bed linens. But he cannot open the chest.

Is the lid stuck? Axel pulls as hard as he can, but the lid does not move. Does the woman want to make a fool of him? Furious, Axel opens the door, shines his light down the stairs, and shrinks back. She is still there! The old woman is sitting on the middle of the stairs. Is she asleep? What is she doing there?

Carefully Axel walks down the creaking stairs. The old woman does not move. "Hello?" cries Axel. He touches the old woman's shoulder and is shocked. The old woman, or what appeared to be an old woman, falls apart. It was a bucket with a broom over which dusters and polishing rags had been hung so that there appeared to be an old woman sitting there.

Axel breathes quickly. Did someone want to play a trick on him, or is he not quite right in the head himself? How could he have been so mistaken? Carefully he steps over the broom and the bucket and proceeds down the stairs. He knocks on the door to the old woman's living room. It remains absolutely quiet. Nobody calls "Come in!" He presses down the handle on the door and shrinks back again. In the middle of the room the landlady is dancing with another old woman. The two old ladies are swaying round by candlelight, bowing to each other and dancing on, always in the same rhythm—but without music!

Axel wants to say that the chest will not open, but he cannot bring himself to say a word. He does not want to disturb the two old ladies who are dancing with complete abandon. Quietly, he goes back to his room.

The bed creaks too. Everything creaks in this house! Why did he not stay in the woods? Why did he have to come down into this misty valley? Who suggested that idea of a bed and an inn to him? Now he is sleeping in his sleeping bag after all because there are no bed linens. Axel keeps turning over and cannot sleep.

Listen! Is someone knocking? Yes, he can hear it very clearly. Someone is knocking on the wooden wall next to his bed. But . . . behind that wall, there is no room and no other house. Behind the wall there is just air . . .

There is another knock. Once, twice, three times! Axel gets up very quietly. If he is to catch the person knocking, he must surprise them. But the floorboards creak so!

Has he driven the knocker away? No, the knocking continues. Almost louder. It seems to be challenging him to do something about it. Axel takes his flashlight from the table and holds it out through the attic window. He allows the light to skim over the roof and the front of the house. Nothing!

He pulls his head back in and listens. There is still knocking! How can there be knocking on a wall without there being anything doing the knocking?

Axel remains standing like that for a while, with his head through the attic window. He listens and shines with his flashlight. Finally he calms down. What can that knocking mean? Ghosts and spirits do not exist. The violin playing came out of a radio, the woman on the stairs was made up of household articles, and there is very probably an ordinary explanation for the weird knocking. Tomorrow, when he knows what the explanation is, he will undoubtedly laugh at himself.

Axel lies down again, but he is not completely calm. The knocking just goes on. "I can't sleep like this!" he cries, furious. He gets up again and searches the roof. There is still nothing to be seen. A cold shiver runs down his spine. Between his bed and the night air, there is only a wooden wall. No one could hide there to play a trick on him, and yet he can hear the knocking.

There is the sound of violin playing. "Anne!" cries Axel and directs his flashlight to the house next door. There she is! The girl is sitting on the middle of the roof with the radio in her hands and she is staring ahead silently. "Anne!" But the girl does not see or hear him. Should he go to her? He hesitates at first but then makes a decision. He cannot sleep anyway. He pulls on his shoes, grabs hold of his flashlight tightly, and walks down the stairs for the second time.

The old woman is sitting there again! Does someone build her up again each time with the bucket, broom, dusters, and polishing rags? He wants to slip past the figure but freezes halfway. This time, he is not mistaken. An old woman he does not know is really sitting there. She smiles at him and puts a finger to her lips. "Ssh!"

"Did you knock?" Axel asks, deliberately loud.

The old woman shakes her head angrily. Then she says again, "Ssh!"

Can she hear something? Is he disturbing her while she is listening? Axel apologizes, walks on down the stairs, and opens the door to the living room. The two other old ladies are still dancing. There is still no music to be heard. They sway and bow. It

must be a primitive dance. Axel thinks he has seen dances like that in documentary films. Could the two old ladies be that old?

Axel stands and watches the two old ladies for a while. Then he has had enough. "There's the sound of knocking in my room!" he cries, as if he has to drown out the music that the two old ladies appear to hear. "There's the sound of knocking all the time! I . . . I can't sleep like this!" In his fear of the two women, he shouts that last bit so loudly that they actually stop dancing and notice him. They each of them take him by the hand and try to draw him into their dancing . . .

"No!" begs Axel, but it is as if he cannot resist. He dares not push the two old women away from him. For a while he dances with them stiffly, and as he does so, he looks at their delighted faces. Finally he pulls himself free and runs outside.

Is he dreaming all this? He is living in the twentieth century, not in the Middle Ages. And even if time has stood still in this valley, what he has experienced in this house could not have been normal in the Middle Ages either.

The neighbor's house! He wanted to go to talk with Anne! Axel switches on his flashlight and shines it up onto the roof. There is no one there anymore. Or is there? . . . Next to the chimney he can see a shadow. Axel walks to the house and directs his flashlight to the shadow next to the chimney.

It is a bird. A big black bird. That must be one of the four ravens that Anne talked about. Axel switches off his flashlight and asks himself whether or not he will knock on Anne's door in the middle of the night.

There is the sound of the beating of wings! The raven has taken off and is flying in circles above Axel's head. Axel tries to follow it with his flashlight but does not succeed. Is someone calling his name? There it is again. "Axel!" That can only be Anne . . . No, it is not Anne. It is not a girl's voice. It is a screeching. It sounds like "Aeksel!" Could it be the raven? Now he can hear loud, shrill laughing. The whole valley is filled with it. It echoes in the mountains, reverberates and blares. There is no end to it. Axel stands paralyzed for a moment and then runs back into the house with the three old women. He would rather have the dancing and knocking than this laughing everywhere around him.

Inside the house everything is quiet and dark. Are the two women no longer dancing? Axel shines his light through the room. There they are, the three of them sitting together. Without looking at each other or at Axel and without uttering even one word, they are sitting there drinking some liqueur or other out of dark glasses.

"Good night!" says Axel. He does not ask about the raven or the laughing. He knows for sure he will get no answer anyway.

"Good night!" As if on command, the three women bow in his direction. Then they suddenly start giggling like little girls who have been up to something.

Axel lies in his sleeping bag again. He holds his arms crossed under his head and waits for the morning. He does not try to fall asleep anymore. He cannot and he does not want to. Not in this valley and not in this house. He is quite sure now that strange things are happening here. Otherwise, he cannot find an explanation for all sorts of things: Anne who reads thoughts and sits on the roof at night, the knocking, the three strange women, the talking raven, and the laughing. He has come to a bewitched valley. That is why it was not marked on his walking map. Yesterday, he would have laughed heartily about this idea of which he is now definitely convinced. He would have considered it all a children's fairy tale and perfect nonsense. But tonight that has changed. He has actually experienced it, not dreamed it. He is not planning on telling anyone because they would not believe him anyway, but it is true!

There is a fluttering sound in the attic window. Axel sits upright. Is it starting again? The fluttering is now in the room, circling above his head. Terrified, Axel switches on his flashlight. No, it cannot be! It is Anne! She is sitting on the table!

"How . . . did you come in?"

Anne does not answer, she just smiles.

Axel is furious. "Has that monstrous raven brought you here?"

"Don't talk like that about Anton," Anne begs softly. "He means you no harm."

"Oh, no? Don't make me laugh! I wish I'd never come down into this valley. Everything is bewitched here."

Anne shakes her head reproachfully. "Not bewitched but enchanted."

"What's the difference?"

"You very well know," says Anne. "You're just angry because you can't understand us."

"Us? So you're not on vacation, then! You belong here, and one day you'll be an old witch just like those downstairs."

"Those down there aren't witches and I am on vacation," Anne protests. "I didn't lie to you. You should have asked where I came from. If you'd done that I might have answered you and then you wouldn't be surprised now."

"All right: where do you come from?"

"It's too late now."

"Why? Tell me where you come from."

"Will you switch off your flashlight?" Anne asks.

"Why?"

"Please switch it off now."

Axel switches off his flashlight. There is a fluttering noise. It moves in the direction of the window and disappears into the darkness.

Axel switches on his flashlight again. Anne has disappeared. She has fooled him.

Angry, Axel goes and lies down again. Where did Anne come from? And how is it that she can fly? Is she perhaps . . . Anton the raven? Anton—Anne. They are alike.

He—or she—means you no harm!

That is what Anne said, but why then do they keep him awake all night? Or would something worse have happened if Anton had meant him harm?

Axel can stand it no longer in his sleeping bag. He looks out of the attic window again to see if it is starting to get light and shrinks back, shocked. The raven is sitting in the gutter on the roof. It holds tight, onto the outside edge with its strong claws and looks at Axel along its big sharp beak.

Go away! Axel wants to shout, but he controls himself. "Are you Anton?" he asks in a friendly manner.

The raven nods its beak up and down.

"And are you . . . Anne too?"

The raven lifts its wings and flies at Axel. Axel wants to hit the bird with his flashlight, but Anton pecks his hand with his beak so hard that he drops the flashlight.

"Why do you do that if you're Anne?" Axel cries and holds his hands in front of his face so that the raven cannot peck him there. But Anton does not want to peck him in the face. He goes back to sit in the gutter and looks up at Axel quietly.

"I've really had enough now!" Axel rolls up his sleeping bag in the dark room and grabs hold of his knapsack. He does not want to wait until it gets light. He is leaving now.

"It's your own fault that Anton was angry," says a voice. Axel turns round. It is Anne. She has his torch in her hand . . .

"Are you that strange bird or not?" cries Axel bitterly.

"Do you believe in fairy tales?"

"Of course not," answers Axel, although he is not so sure anymore.

"Why do you ask, then?"

"Because I . . . Oh, I'm sick to death of everything."

Axel takes his flashlight and his knapsack and walks quickly down the stairs. This time there is no old woman sitting on the stairs, not one made of flesh and blood and not one made of a bucket, a broom, and old dusters either. There is no dancing in the living room. There is no one at all. Axel takes out his wallet and lays the money for the night's stay on the table.

Was there a scratching noise there? Axel allows the light from the flashlight to glide across the walls, against which all kinds of old-fashioned things are standing.

At first he sees nothing, but then he discovers three ravens on the cupboard. They are looking at him and appear to be laughing at him.

"Do you want to dance?" he shouts, looking for something to throw at the ravens.

But suddenly Anne is standing in front of him again. She spreads out her arms and says, "Don't."

"Oh well, what's the use anyway? I'm certain the old women couldn't care less."

Axel runs out of the house and remains standing, dazed. It is no longer night. The valley is bathed in sunlight, birds are chirping, and a warm stillness hangs over the meadows. He reflects and is dissatisfied with himself. Actually, nobody in this house has done anything to him. If the three women want to dance, they should do so. If they want to change themselves into ravens every now and again, it is up to them. And if there is knocking on the walls of their house without there being anyone there to knock, that is not necessarily their fault. It is only because of his own fear that he has behaved so outrageously.

He wants to go back to apologize to Anne and the three ravens, and he turns round. But what has happened? There is no house anymore. Just an old barn. Bewildered, Axel stares at the dilapidated building. He has just walked outside, has he not? Can the house have been changed into a barn behind his back so quickly? It must have been, for on top of the roof four ravens are sitting looking at him seriously.

"I'm sorry," Axel calls up. "I'm sorry I was so angry."

The four ravens show no reaction at all. "Which one of you is Anton?" Axel wants to know.

Did the raven on the right move its beak up and down, or is he just imagining it? Axel is doubtful but decides to greet that raven in particular after all. When he has done that and turns round again, he suddenly sees Anne's radio lying at his feet. He picks it up and turns it on. There is the sound of violin music! The same music that Anne always listened to . . .

"Thank you," Axel calls up to the roof. But there is no one there to receive his thanks anymore. No people and no ravens.

Eiko Kadono

The Mirror

Mom! Have you seen my new hat?" I called loudly, rushing downstairs.

"You were trying it on in front of the mirror last night, weren't you, Ariko?"

I looked into the next room on the way, but my hat wasn't there. Where could it be? If I didn't hurry, I'd miss the bus. I had to be waiting there when Hiroshi came.

On the way home from school the other day, Hiroshi and Isamu were walking in front of me. I quietly moved closer to them and could hear Hiroshi talking.

"On Sunday, I'm going to the video game store in Machida. Why don't you come along, Isamu? Second-hand games are really cheap there, you know. Come on, keep me company for a change," he pressed.

"Naw, I don't think I can," Isamu said, looking unhappy.

"How come?"

"No money." Isamu grimaced to cover his embarrassment, and started to run. "Maybe some other time. See you later!" He waved and disappeared around the corner.

Hiroshi snorted in disappointment and broke into a run.

Watching him go, I made up my mind that I would go to the video game store in Machida. I knew that store. I'd go and wait in front, and when Hiroshi arrived, I'd act surprised and pretend it was a coincidence. My heart began to pound at the thought.

Hiroshi was the tallest boy in our class. He was quite handsome, with long lashes, like the heroes of popular comic stories we were always reading. The girls had their eyes on him constantly, especially Keiko and Yasuko. Whenever they had time, they seemed to be gossiping about him.

Of course, I was no exception. I was drawn to Hiroshi too. I decided I wouldn't tell anyone I was planning to go to Machida. Little by little, I'd make friends with Hiroshi, and secretly, unknown to everybody, I'd have him all for myself. Then, when the secret got out, wouldn't everyone be surprised! I could almost hear them tittering about it now. I was nearly dancing on air at the very thought of their reaction.

On Sunday, I thought, I'll wear my dress with the red polka dots and the white hat Mom bought me. I'll blow-dry my hair to make it silky and bouncy, the way I liked it best.

So last night I'd done a little rehearsal, putting on the hat and turning this way and that. Mom had a knowing smile on her face when she said to Dad, "I'm glad I bought that hallway mirror, now that we have a stylish girl in the house. She's already twelve, after all."

"I suppose so," said Dad with a frown, "but I get a scare when I open the door late at night and come face to face with myself."

"The truth about Dad," I said melodramatically, "is in the mirror! Maybe what surprises you is the reflection of what you really are. There must be something suspicious about you," I teased him. "Suppose what surprises you is the mirror showing what you really are? . . . No, I'm only joking! Just joking," I protested as Dad glared at me.

But I couldn't help feeling I was right.

Mom's eyes twinkled as she chided, "Goodness, Ariko, you shouldn't talk like that to your father." She turned to Dad. "Dear, I'm sure you'll get used to the mirror after a while."

"Well, Dad," I said, "if you don't like being welcomed home

by the spooky mirror, come home earlier—while Mom and I are awake." And I went back to admiring myself. Yes, I thought, preening, I do look pretty cute.

That was only last night, and now the hat was nowhere to be seen. Could I have left it on top of the chest of drawers in my room? I started to run back upstairs to check again, but something stopped me. It was me, reflected in the mirror, but grinning, with a snide sort of smile. That's strange, I thought, and then I caught my breath. The me in the mirror was holding the hat.

"Oh, there it is!," I exclaimed, and without thinking I stretched out my hand. Suddenly my hand was grasped and yanked so that my whole body was pulled forward into a spin and then thrown out somewhere.

"Mom, I found my hat, so I'm going."

It was the girl with the hat who spoke, and she was moving toward the front door.

"Wait, wait!" I called out, flailing my arms desperately.

Looking back, the girl smiled wryly and said, "Sorry about that," and then she ran out the door.

That was *my* face, no mistake. But . . . why? *I'm* here.

My mom's cheerful farewell echoed down the hallway. "See you later! Take care, now."

I didn't understand what was happening. But then I thought, I have to go after that girl and stop her.

I got up but immediately ran full force into some obstacle. I moved forward again, and again I hit something. I couldn't get through. Yet the hallway and the rest of the house were right there in front of me. I could see the back of the sofa where we sat to watch television and past that the entrance. To one side was the kitchen, where Mom was washing the dishes.

"Mom! Mother!" I screamed, beating the barrier wildly with my fists. But she didn't even turn around. I tried again, throwing my whole weight into the effort. But I bounced back and crumpled into a heap. Gasping, I huddled there for some time.

Mom turned around, wiping her hands with her apron, and came up to the mirror. She brought her face close to the glass.

"Mom, it's me! Here!"

Again I pounded at the mirror. But Mom obviously couldn't see or hear me. She looked at herself, smoothing an eyebrow with her forefinger and pursing her lips as if putting on lipstick.

Then suddenly I realized where I was. I was *inside* the mirror! I must have been pulled in when my arm was yanked a little while before. But whoever heard of a person being inside a mirror? If I really was inside the mirror, the girl with the hat must have pulled me in. Yet that girl's face was unmistakably my own. If that was me, why was I here? And who was that girl?

Mom went upstairs humming and soon came back down dressed to go out. I could hear the front door open and the key turn in the lock outside. Through a slit in the curtains, I caught a glimpse of her walking toward the main street. It was Sunday. Dad should be home, I thought. No, now I remembered: he went out early in the morning to play golf.

I began to think that if I'd got into the mirror, there must be a way out. I began to grope at the invisible wall before me, but suddenly I realized with horror that I could not see my own hands. I raised both arms and looked hard, but I couldn't see them. Alarmed, I looked down at my feet. They were invisible. My heart began to pound and the blood drained out of my head.

"No! Oh, it can't be true! Help me!" I began to scream hysterically, groping frantically for different parts of my body. But I could feel them there, my arms, my chest. I just couldn't see them.

All I could see was an inky blackness.

I looked behind me. It was black there too; total darkness. I couldn't even see my shadow. I was completely alone and scared. Was I going crazy? On the other side, the room outside the mirror was bright, but not a ray of light from that side shone into my side of the mirror.

Finally I heard the clank of the key turning in the lock and the front door being flung open.

"How come it's so hot in here? I can't stand it!"

The girl lunged through the door and dropped the hat on a chair, grabbing the air conditioner's remote control. She stood right in front of the cool air streaming forth, raising and flapping her skirt to let in the breeze. She didn't seem to care that her underpants were showing. She got herself a drink of water in the kitchen and came over to the mirror, sticking her chin out at me meanly.

"Well, aren't you looking the frightened one!" she exclaimed.

"What? You can see me!" I said.

"That's right. Once I'm on this side, you can see me—who is yourself—but if I don't come up close, you can't see yourself. It's all up to me whether you see yourself or not!"

I tried holding up my hand again. Now I could see my palm, shining whitely in the darkness. I quickly checked again. Now I could see my feet and knees and stomach. With a rush of relief I felt for my arms.

"If you want to be able to see yourself, you have to treat me better, you know. Hey! Listen, there's something I want to tell you. I did go to Machida and met Hiroshi instead of you. Everything went just fine. Don't worry about a thing." She spoke with a snide slur.

"I don't care about that. Just get me out of here!" I shouted, thrashing about.

"Now, don't get yourself all worked up!" she said, her mouth forming a crooked grin. "I'm going to hang around out here for a while. I'm going to change your whole life. I'll make your sweetie-pie life even more sweetie-pie . . . "

"I don't need your help. Just what is going on? What are you trying to do? Come on, explain. Why am I in here, anyway?"

"I grabbed your hand on purpose." She giggled meanly, showing her open palm and slowly waving it. "You're so dimwitted, you obviously didn't realize it, but every time you looked in the mirror, you totally ignored me. You only saw what you *wanted* to see, posing like a 'good girl' all the time, even though in fact you're really shamelessly self-centered. People may pat you on the back and praise you, but it makes me sick. I was horrified every time I saw you acting like that. I made up my mind to give you a hard time when I got the chance."

"That's no concern of mine. It doesn't make sense! Now, get me out of here right away!"

"One of these days . . . maybe, sometime," she said haughtily. "When I think it's time, I'll let you out. So you'd better just wait quietly until then. What's with the tears? Well, that's a new one—when did I ever see you cry before? Do you think you can scare me by crying, young lady? Whether you get out or not is up to me. All I have to do is take hold of your hand."

"Okay, then, quick! Come on, please!" I didn't want to admit that I was at her mercy, but I stretched out my right hand.

"I'd never take your hand now, silly. I just got here! I finally broke loose of you! So I'm not about to give you my hand anytime soon." She hid her hands behind her and then took one and then two steps away from the mirror, smiling all the time.

Mom came through the front door. "Oh, Ariko, you're back already. That was a quick trip. Wasn't it hot out there today?" Taking a deep breath, Mom put a large shopping bag on the sofa. "Did you have fun in Machida?"

"Nothing special," said the girl in a sullen voice.

"Did you buy anything?"

"Nothing in particular."

"That doesn't tell me much. You did have a good time, I hope. Who did you go with?"

The girl didn't answer.

"Ariko. I asked you a question . . . "

"What does it matter who I went with? It has nothing to do with you, Mom. Why do you ask so many questions?" The girl made no attempt to hide her snort of contempt.

Mom's hand stopped on the way to the refrigerator door. She turned in amazement to stare at her.

"Ariko, dear, what happened to you?"

"I *said*, 'Nothing in particular.' It was fun enough." The girl threw me a look and then, to change the subject, poked her hand into Mom's shopping bag.

"What did you buy . . . wow! You bought me this blouse, didn't you?"

I could hear her ripping the paper wrapper open, and pulling out a light blue blouse, she pranced toward the mirror, dangling it in front of her.

"What do you think? Isn't it nice?" she said to me in a low voice as she modeled the blouse.

It was a beautiful color. Mom must have bought the blouse because she knew I had wanted something in that color for a long time.

"Show me," I said, putting my hands out in front of me.

"Here." She started to hold up the blouse close to the mirror and then in a flurry snatched it back. "Oh! Oh, no, you don't! That was close!" She quickly drew back and turned away in the other direction.

"So, do you like it?" Mom asked.

"Mom, you know I don't like this color. It's like any old blouse. Go back and exchange it for something more flashy." Her tone was petulant, totally different from a minute ago when she had stood showing off her prize in front of me.

"What, you don't like it?" Mom was taken by surprise.

"I'm so bored with this color. Everything's this blue. I'm not a kid anymore, you know." Throwing the shirt at Mom, she thumped noisily up the stairs. Shocked and speechless, Mom didn't move for a moment.

"Goodness, what's happened to her?" she said softly, gazing after her. Once, talking on the phone to a friend, Mom had said, "Ariko's never been a problem. Well, she's caught a cold now and then, maybe, but we always get along. My husband teases us for being like twins." Now, that confidence was gone. She looked bewildered at the sudden change in her daughter.

Mom started to make coffee. I wondered what I had done to deserve such a cruel turn of events. Tears welled up in my eyes. I hadn't been hungry since morning and didn't have to go to the bathroom, but for some reason my tears kept flowing.

Enveloped by darkness, I huddled there like a baby, clasped my knees, and sobbed.

"You should just give up."

The sudden sound of a voice speaking in the darkness was eerie. At once distant and very close, it was a boy's voice.

"Who are you?" Startled, I straightened and looked around. Again I asked, this time with more urgency in my voice, "Who is it? Answer me!"

"My name is Kazuo."

"Where . . . where are you?"

"Right here, beside you."

"Where? I can't see a thing."

"No, I'm invisible."

"But you can see me, right?"

"No."

"Oh, no! Until just a minute ago, I could . . . " My voice trailed off as I saw that my body had disappeared again.

"You can see yourself only when she stands in front of the mirror. When we enter here, we have no form," said the boy's voice.

"What do you mean, 'when we enter here'?" I was trembling from head to foot. "You mean you too, were pulled into the mirror?"

"Yes. Yes, but it was a long time ago."

"What do you mean, 'a long time'?"

"It'll be about twenty-five years now."

"What! Did you say twenty-five years? Oh, no!" I let out a scream.

"Wow! You've still got spunk." Kazuo was chuckling. He sounded a little less eerie than before. The voice was now that of an ordinary boy, but it had no expression, like someone reading from a book.

"In my case, it was a test paper. I'd gotten a really bad grade, and just as I was about to tear it up so my mother wouldn't find it, the me in the mirror grabbed it. When I lunged after it, he pulled me in."

"He looked just like you?"

"Yeah, exactly. Except he was a really good kid."

"So you've been in here ever since? No, that just couldn't be! You must be making this up."

"I wish it weren't true . . . But unfortunately, I am still here. He was very careful. Saying all the while that he'd let me out eventually, he never held out his hand even once. Then, six years later, he was run over by a train and killed. I've remained the same age ever since—I don't age, no matter how much time passes. Probably I can't even die. And there is no chance I'll ever be able to cross back to the other side. Pretty depressing story, huh?"

"But there was your mother. Didn't she help you?"

"Hardly," he snickered. "She had my other side right there with her. And besides, he was suddenly such a smart, good boy. He didn't talk back or misbehave. Day in, day out, Mother looked so happy. She was overjoyed with her son. So when he died, you should have seen how she grieved. My father had died and I don't remember him at all. Around three years after that my mother remarried—a guy from the place where she worked. And she moved out, leaving this old mirror behind."

"Just a minute!" I was beside myself to think of what that meant. "You mean you've been in here ever since?"

"I can't even see my mother."

I turned back toward the house in which I had been moving about freely until this very morning. The rays of the evening sun were shining through the clouded glass in the front entranceway. Mom was at the kitchen sink, starting to fix dinner. I could hear the sound of water running and Mom's humming as she worked.

"Mom! Mom!" My tears gushed forth.

"You're lucky you can still cry," said Kazuo. "After a while it gets hard to talk, and you forget words."

"Oh, no! Not me!" I said desperately. "I'm getting out of here. No matter what it takes."

"Well, you'll have to beg that girl for it," said Kazuo.

Mopping my tears with my skirt, I raised my head. There were a lot of things I wanted to ask this boy Kazuo.

"So you must have come into my house with this mirror."

"That's right. But I've been all over the place. After a while, the person who bought my house sold the mirror to an antique dealer. It was bought first by a boutique and later by an actress, then some kind of scholar. And then the antique shop where your mother bought it. I moved every time a house was redecorated or rebuilt."

"And are you the only one left inside like this?"

"Actually, there was someone else. A girl. The daughter of the scholar. By the way, how old are you?"

"Twelve."

"That's what I thought. You know, it's really strange. That girl was twelve too. And I was twelve."

"And what happened to that girl?"

"Strange things started to happen, and then . . . "

"Like what?"

"The girl out there started acting odd. She stopped talking to the others in the family—or anybody. She stopped going to school. She'd just sit in front of the mirror and daydream, but carefully, keeping her hands well away. And then at night, she'd turn this way, put on lipstick, and then get up and go out somewhere. Her mother and father would forbid her, but she'd go anyway, and raise a ruckus if they tried to stop her . . . Come to think of it, I just realized while I was telling all this—the ones on the other side of the mirror all go crazy somehow. In my case, he got run over by a train, the scholar's daughter went mad, and that girl who took your place is pretty weird too."

"But yours was a good boy, wasn't he? Did you say he was really smart?"

"Yes, he looked just like me, but unlike me, he was really clever, and he was nice to my mom and all. But then one day, when he saw the train coming, he jumped off the platform and started walking toward the train, all very calm and smiling. That's not normal, you know. So everyone said it was suicide. Maybe there was something, something that went haywire, inside that kid. That's the only reason I can think of. And that girl, you know, she was really a sweet-looking, good kid, and then she suddenly started acting crazy like that. She threw a marble clock at her father and hurt him."

"You're kidding!" I remembered the cold, noncommittal answers the girl had made to my mother's questions earlier, the way she had seemed to have a chip on her shoulder. Then suddenly I felt a cold shiver go down my spine. "So what happened to that girl? Where is she?"

"Her parents decided they'd better put her in a different school. Eventually it was decided that they would move to her mother's home in the country, and they disposed of all their household furniture. On the day they handed the mirror over to the shop dealer, the girl out there turned her back without so much as a look in our direction, and left. The girl on this side cried and screamed with all her might, but there was nothing she could do. And so we were handed over to the antique shop."

"And then what happened? She's obviously not here anymore."

"Well, for about ten days she went on crying. But gradually she calmed down and then finally, murmuring, 'I'm going, I have to see if there's anything out there,' she disappeared. I tried to stop her, but . . . I wondered why she went. At least here we can see the goings on in the world outside. She might even see her counterpart, or her family, again one day. My me isn't around anymore, but I believe something might happen that could free me from the mirror. Help can only come from that bright world, so I'm waiting for my chance. After all, I *really belong* to the world out there."

He paused and then went on. "If you sit very still in this darkness, you begin to think you can hear something. When the house is quiet, try listening. From somewhere deep, deep down, it sounds as if many people are calling out to each other. The sound is very faint, though. I think that girl was drawn away by that sound, and I sometimes think I'll just give up and walk away from here—I've even taken a step or two into the darkness. But you have to be really brave, you know—it's pitch black! It's so scary—and you might melt into nothing in the darkness. I just can't do it."

"No! No! No!" I began to cry again, blubbering out loud. "I'm only twelve! I want to move around out there in the bright light!"

"I envy you, still being able to cry."

"What, you can't cry?"

"You can cry because there are still people you love out there, whom you can see and hear. When you don't have anyone . . . You know, I'm really glad you came; I feel some warmth coming back into my body."

I could hear the sound of long-suppressed tears and a faint sniffling. Kazuo's voice was now almost back to normal.

"Hey! Hey, you-who-is-me." The voice came from somewhere above, and I looked up.

"You're looking pretty pale and wan. All tired out, huh? Well, let me tell you, you've got a long wait ahead of you, so get a grip on yourself." She shook her head and with a proud gesture ran her fingers through her hair.

I was totally exhausted. Three days had passed. Now and then that girl would come up to the mirror, just like before, and tease and heckle me. Each time I strained every nerve as I watched for the chance to grab her hand, but the effort left me weary.

"You know, today Hiroshi is coming here," she announced.

"Where?" I doubted my ears.

"Here to the house. I invited him to tea," she said coyly. "See how clever I am. I used my head, I tell you. The difference between you and me, you know, is here and here." She pointed first to her heart and then to her head.

"If Keiko or Yasuko knew, wouldn't they be surprised! And to think, they have a crush on him!" she snickered.

The door chime rang.

The girl ran over and opened the door. Hiroshi came through the door. I could see his face over her shoulder. Tight-lipped and eyes glaring, he looked extremely tense.

"Oh, come on in," said the girl.

"I haven't come for fun," said Hiroshi. "I just came to set things straight."

"Set what straight?"

"That I'm not going to spend any more time with you."

"Well, that's pretty final."

"I almost decided not to come, but I think you ought to know how I feel about this."

"What are you talking about?"

"That I did no such thing as try to steal something at the game store. You said if I didn't come over here, you'd spread the story around school that I was shoplifting. But I didn't do it!"

"Ha! You're lying. Don't you remember we agreed to do it together?" Her body swayed slightly.

Hiroshi's eyes flashed. "When did we ever agree to do anything? I never thought you were such a troublemaker, Ariko." His voice rose to a shout. "How can you do such a thing?"

The girl's voice rose to match his. "You can shout all you like, but I know you're really a coward."

"Ariko! What's going on?" Mom's voice called from upstairs.

"Nothing, Mom." The harsh siren suddenly turned into the sweet daughter. "Hiroshi's come over to visit."

"I'm leaving." Hiroshi turned away.

"Okay, you can go home. But I'll see you tomorrow at school, and you'd better be prepared."

"For what?" He turned back toward her, glaring.

"What on earth is the matter?" Mom was coming down the stairs. "Quarreling? My goodness, you're not little kids anymore."

Trembling with anger, Hiroshi appealed to my mother. "Mrs. Mori, Ariko's gone too far. I won't let her get away with it. Listen to what she did. The other day I went to the computer game store in Machida, and as I passed the cash register, an alarm went off. Somehow, a game I hadn't paid for got into my bag, and the shopkeeper accused me of shoplifting. But I tell, you, Mrs. Mori, I didn't do it. I don't do things like that! Then I saw Ariko on the other side of the store. Since I knew Ariko from school and thought she was nice, I hoped she'd help me get out of that mess. But do you know what she did? She said, 'I'm sorry. We agreed to do it together. I took one too,' and she pulled a game out of her pocket. And then she started weeping and saying, 'Hiroshi kept saying, "Let's do it, let's do it," until I . . .' But listen, Mrs. Mori, I absolutely did not do it. How can she do such a thing to me!"

"Hiroshi, how can you lie like that?" the girl shouted. "You were the one who said, 'Let's do it together—I always do it, so it'll be okay.' How can you put all the blame on me like that? You're the one who's the coward!"

"What in heaven's name . . . " Mom looked stunned, as if her face had frozen. In the mirror, too, I was so surprised I thought I'd stop breathing. To say that Hiroshi had shoplifted! Never. I knew he'd never do such a thing.

Hiroshi continued, "I've been to that store many times and the shopkeepers knew me, so they went easy on us. The manager said, 'I suppose you two just couldn't resist. We'll let you off this time, but next time we'll call the police.' And after really bawling us out, they let us go.

"But then today at school, Ariko told me she was going to tell everybody. I told her that if she did that, I'd tell them about her too. But then she said, 'Oh! I didn't do anything! What, are you going to lie again?' She's crazy. I won't believe a word she says. And then she says if I don't want the story to get out I have to tell everybody that I'm in love with her and am going to visit her at home. Over my dead body—I'll never say anything like that! The whole thing is crazy!"

"Ariko. Is all this true?" Mom's voice was trembling.

"Do you think I'd do anything like that, Mom? Hiroshi's just lying," the girl said, trying to look innocent.

"I am *not* lying," Hiroshi declared firmly.

"Okay, okay. So why don't you go on home. So I won't tell on you. I won't say you were a thief. Okay?" She made it sound as if she were doing him a favor.

"I didn't do it!" he shouted again, incensed.

Mom's voice was trembling. "Hiroshi, Ariko's not been herself lately. She's suddenly become very angry all the time, and I've been rather worried about her myself."

"There's nothing wrong with me," snapped the girl.

"I'll talk things over carefully with Ariko later, Hiroshi, so could you forget about this for today? Ariko, tell him you're sorry."

"No!"

"Ariko!" Mom's voice rose in warning.

"Okay, I guess there's no end to this. I'm going home." He sounded a little calmer as he ran out.

On the verge of tears, Mom turned to the girl. "Ariko, what is the meaning of all this? I can't believe you would do such a thing. Even if somebody encouraged you to do it, I could never believe that you would shoplift."

"So you believe Hiroshi instead of me, Mom? So that's how it is, is it? I think I have a headache. I'm going to bed." And the girl headed up the stairs.

"Wait! Just wait a minute, Ariko!"

Mom stared at the girl's face. With a penetrating look, she said, "Are you really Ariko? You're acting like someone completely different . . ."

"I'm your daughter, all right. If you hate me so much, slap me, or you can even kill me. It happens all the time." She spat this out and then ran up the stairs. I could hear the sound of my bedroom door slamming shut. Mom sank down exhausted where she stood and gazed upward as if to hold in the tears that brimmed in her eyes.

I felt as if my heart would break. Just who could that girl be? That girl who looked exactly like me—she had called me "You-who-is-me" . . . What could she have meant?

Then Dad came home. He was almost always too late coming home from work to join us for dinner, and it was unusual for all three members of the family to eat together. Both Mom and the girl were silent.

Dad was in a good mood. "Wow! Beef stew! Mom's stew is the best. This makes me want some wine. Would you bring us a bottle, dear?"

Gazing nervously at the girl, Mom slowly answered, "That's a good idea. Ariko, you're closest, could you bring over the wine?"

"Bring it yourself," she snapped with disdain.

Darting a startled look at Mom, Dad turned to the girl. "What's the matter with you? Here we are, about to enjoy a meal together for a change, and you act like this. Come on, let's try to enjoy ourselves, okay?"

"You say 'for a change.' Don't you think it's asking too much to leave us alone all the time and then come back and be treated nicely? Yes, it's been a long time since we ate together, so don't you think you should be a little more humble?" She rolled her eyes in spite.

Dad's face flushed and his hands began to tremble. "How dare you talk to me like that!"

"All right. I'll shut up. I'll do anything you say. I'm just here to follow your orders. Isn't that right? It's a real nightmare to eat with this kind of family!" Slamming her chopsticks down on the table, she stood up and headed for the stairs.

Dad stood up to go after her but stopped, his eyes following her. He didn't really believe what he had just witnessed.

Mom tried to intercede. "Now, dear, let's keep calm. Why don't you sit down? She's at a difficult age, you know. And you're not completely free of blame, yourself."

"What? How am I to blame?"

"Well, don't you always tell us you have 'work, work, work'? You never take time to be with Ariko these days. When was the last time you talked to her at all?" Mom's voice gradually grew more accusing.

"That's nonsense! It's my job—to support the two of you!" Now Dad was getting angry.

"You always say it's for our sakes, but how do you know that's what we'd be most grateful for? I can't think of anything more presumptuous. If being out every night of the week and spending your weekends with your company friends is for our sakes, you don't have to do it anymore for us. It's no wonder Ariko's started misbehaving. Today at school she threatened a friend in the most unthinkable way. It's terrible!"

"So you've both decided it's all my fault. I left everything in the household up to you, believing that you were capable of handling it. Have I ever complained about the way you ran things? Haven't I left you to do exactly what you wanted, free to use the money I earned the way you saw fit? Did you ever consult me before you bought something? Take that gloomy old mirror. I don't care whether it's an antique or whatever you make it out to be, but I don't like it."

"Well, excuse me, but it was you, by the way, who said it would be nice to have a mirror in the hallway. I just acted on your suggestion. Oh, never mind, I'll phone the shop tomorrow and have them take it back."

"You do whatever you want." Dad got up noisily, shuffled into his shoes, and left the house.

How could things have reached such a pass? Ever since that girl had pulled me into the mirror, something seemed wrong with both my mother and father. Now it looked as if the whole household was going haywire. Suddenly I felt very cold all over. Mom's words came back to me: tomorrow she would call and have the mirror taken away. This mirror!

"Kazuo! Kazuo!" I called out in a panic, searching around me in the darkness.

"I'm right here," the voice said very near me.

"Mom says she's going to return the mirror to the shop."

"Yes, I heard."

"Where will I be taken? If I'm separated from that girl, I'll never get out of here!"

"Yes, that's true."

"Isn't there something I can do? Come on, tell me!"

"If I knew, I wouldn't be here . . . "

"But he died. There's no one to pull you back anyway."

"I wish you'd have a little more respect for my feelings." Kazuo sounded hurt. "Now listen, no matter how you scream and carry on, what can't be done can't be done. People go their separate ways, or die, eventually. You're old enough to know that."

"Oh, no!" I collapsed, crying.

Then I heard Mom talking on the phone. "I'm sorry to cause you so much trouble, but you know the mirror I bought the other day? I wonder if you'd be willing to take it back? My husband says it's too big, you see. At half the price? That would be fine. Tomorrow? I'll be at home in the morning. Fine. I'll be waiting."

After putting down the receiver, Mom turned around and looked long and hard at the mirror. Her face was haggard, with circles around her eyes and cheeks sunken. In the space of only one day, her face had undergone unbelievable changes.

Suddenly the girl was standing in front of me. "Did you know? They're going to return this mirror to the shop?"

I nodded silently.

"I'd like to do you the favor of changing places, but I don't want to go back in there either." She threw out her arms and shrugged. "That's the way it is. Put up with it, okay?"

Her attitude made me mad. I felt as if my blood would boil, but I tried to keep my feelings in check. I said calmly, "Which one of us will have to put up with it, I wonder. The family is a mess anyway. It's going to break apart. Mom and Dad aren't getting along. And then there's you, with your heart as black as the devil. You're going to go on living like that, with everyone in the family on a different wavelength, sniping at each other all the time? Good luck!"

"Black as the devil, you say? Hah! I won't be a kid forever, you know. I'll manage all right."

"That's impossible! Because you took over everything!"

The girl turned away sullenly. "Don't act so superior." She tried to laugh at me, but her face suddenly betrayed fear and lost its spitefulness. "I didn't want to take over. I just wanted to get away from you for a change—to find out what it would be like without you." She murmured as if talking to herself.

Morning came. I crouched down and put my face on my knees, gazing intently at the house visible before me. I could hear the sound of the newspaper man's bicycle. The sun began to shine through the kitchen window and gradually spread through the rooms.

Mom came down the stairs and started to make breakfast. She was making coffee. She was frying eggs. I realized that these ordinary things that had been such a routine part of my day, no longer would be.

Mom made her own breakfast only and began to eat. Dad came down ready to go to work. He left without saying a word to her. Then the girl came down the stairs.

"I'm not going to school today," she said.

"Please yourself," said Mom sharply.

"Hello!" called a man peering in at the door. "I've come to take the mirror."

"There it is, if you wouldn't mind taking it down," said Mom.

"I'm sorry if you didn't like it, ma'am. It's very old but a first-class mirror, the kind of thing you can't find much anymore."

"Yes, but my husband said he didn't like it, and when he says something like that, there's no changing his mind." She didn't smile.

The man stared for a moment in amazement but then got hold of himself. He slipped off his shoes to enter the house and crossed the hallway to unfasten the mirror.

I braced myself and then called out, "Kazuo!"

There was no answer, only the huge shadow of the man blocking my view of the house. He raised his arm and began to unscrew the mirror from the wall. I could hear the sound of the screws turning.

Then I saw the girl watching. From a distance, but watching, her eyes flitting this way again and again, she was looking but pretending not to.

Gathering all my strength, I screamed, "Do you really want it to end like this?" But she quickly turned away and hid behind the wall. The mirror shifted and was taken off the wall and set on the floor.

"Kazuo! I'm . . . I'm leaving, I'm going," I shouted.

This time he answered, "Don't go! You mustn't go! If you go, you could miss your chance. That other girl never did come back. It's better to stay here. And you never know who else might come in. It might get to be quite lively in here. Please stay!"

"No! I can't stand it. Even if I stay, what good is it? Did you see her, she just abandoned me, as if it meant nothing to her at all!

I give up on her. It doesn't matter what, I have to get out of here."

I closed my eyes, took a deep breath, and plunged into the darkness.

"Don't leave me all alone again!" Kazuo's voice trailed after me.

For a moment I thought my body had melted into the darkness. It was deep, seemingly liquid. Nothing moved. But from far, far away, I thought I could hear something: voices mingling, whispering, murmuring, seemed to call to me. I felt as if I had melted and was flowing toward those faint sounds. So it is all over, I thought, I am going to be blotted out.

Then, little by little, I felt something stirring near me. It was like a breeze, a slight current of air, and then far, far ahead, a tiny point of light appeared. Hastily, as if gathering up lost parts of myself, I tried to find my body. I could feel myself. I even felt a faint strength. Relying on the warmth of that strength, I struggled to wade through the darkness toward that point of light. I was determined to reach it.

The ray of light gradually broadened and then grew stronger, lightening up my surroundings slightly. There—I could see the gate of our house. The front door, the door was open. The man in overalls carrying the mirror out of the door. I started running.

"Wait! Could you just wait a minute, mister!" The girl's cry from inside the house was close to a scream, and then she flew out of the door. I ran, holding my right hand out in front of me. She came running, her hand held out. Our hands touched and gripped. We came back together again.

The antique shop dealer said, "Oh! Miss. What is it? Did you forget something?"

"Oh! Oh, no, nothing. Thank you," I answered. She answered.

That night, my father came home early. He opened the wine

himself and poured some for Mom too.

"Oh, it's delicious!" Mom took one sip and let out her breath. "I guess you're right. It's better not to have a mirror there in the hall. It was kind of oppressive, as if one was always being watched."

"See, that's what I meant. But never mind. I'll buy you a better one one of these days," said Dad, as if nothing had happened.

But I said, "I don't need a big mirror there. The one in the bathroom is enough for me."

I checked my mom's face and then my father's. Nothing seemed to have changed. But I had seen the other side of my mother and father. I knew that I would go on living with this mother, this father, and that girl who was the other side of myself.

About a month later, I happened to pass by the antique shop. When I peeked into the shop, the shopkeeper saw me.

"Did you sell that mirror already?" I asked, my heart fluttering a bit.

"Yes. It was a good mirror. I put on a new frame and sold it very quickly. Would you have liked it, young lady?"

"No, no. I was just curious." I backed out politely and walked away quickly.

So now where had Kazuo gone? Had he ever gone into the darkness? Wherever he was, I couldn't help feeling he was right here quite close to me. Kazuo would be watching over me from now on. I would always think that, even though I couldn't see him.

Now, whenever I see a mirror, I just put my hands behind my back. I never want to be pulled in there again. But then, I'll never be twelve again either.

Paul Biegel

The Ivory Door

(According to a medieval legend)

He can't help it," said the nurse. "It's because of that rattling thunderclap."

"Yes, that's what you always say."

"It's true! I was there. When he was born. It happened at that exact moment. When he appeared, so to speak. A rattling thunder-clap. The whole castle shook."

"Then you'd expect him to have become a timid boy. After a crack like that."

"Timid! Huh!" they cried. For timid was the last thing that you would call the boy. He was a daredevil, a boy who slid down the banisters, who called out "boo" in dark alcoves, banged on doors, ran down long corridors, pounded on the stairs, danced on the beds, climbed on the roofs, jumped in the ponds, a boy who appeared at breakfast with golden curls and rosy cheeks and wearing a perfectly pressed pair of trousers, and in the evening, full of tears, scratches, bruises, and bumps, had to be scrubbed in the bath with soap, like a black beetle. His name was Prince Darrell. He was called Prince Daredevil. But the lady-in-waiting, the nanny who scrubbed him with soap every evening, called him "gracious child." She was a lady of noble birth, Baroness Von Wetering Tetering, but he called her Minny. And that was allowed, for she was so fond of her gracious child.

One evening, covered in soap bubbles, he asked suddenly, "Minny, what's the ivory door?"

The sponge in the baroness's hand stopped halfway, she was

so shocked by the question. "Whatever makes you ask a thing like that, gracious child?" she asked, and her voice trembled.

He could hear that and he shouted, "You're not allowed to say, are you? About the door. But it exists! It's somewhere here in the cellar and there's something funny about it. Something scary. And I know about it anyway. And I'm going to look for it. And I'm going to open it. Look what's behind it. A ghost? Yes, is it that?"

She sat trembling on the edge of the bath; the soap dripped in colored bubbles from the sponge in her hand, and she did not know what to say.

"Ha ha, Minny!" he cried, his legs kicking and splashing. "Ha ha! I can see that you know. You must tell me!"

But she did not do that and he turned away from her crossly. When she brought him to bed, he pulled the blankets over his head and did not want to be told a story.

The Baroness Von Wetering Tetering reported it to his father the king immediately.

"Oh, God!" sighed the king. "Have we reached that stage?"

And the queen sighed, "Mother Mary! Now we've lost him."

The ivory door was deep down in the castle, in the wall of the side cellar where no one ever came; what was behind it, nobody knew. A cupboard, a room, a hall, a ravine, a crocodile, a hell-fire, a well with water as black as ink, a pitfall with iron spikes at the bottom—one thing was sure: whoever went through the ivory door never came back. The brother of the king's great-grandfather was the last in the family to have risked taking the step; nothing was ever heard of him again. Since then, the ivory door was locked up with a steel padlock, the key of which was kept by the king, on his belt during the day and under his pillow at night. "But now," said the king, "we'll have to put a guard in front. Henry, take care of it."

Henry bowed low and went to make sure that a guard came to stand in front of the ivory door behind which lurked doom.

"Tomorrow we'll tell him," said the king, and after breakfast the next morning he took Prince Darrell aside and began, "Son, listen now."

"Yes, Father, the ivory door," answered the prince. "I'm going to keep on searching until I find it and then I'm going to walk through it."

"You're not going through it," said the king.

"Why not?"

"Because I say so."

"But what's behind it, then?"

"I don't know, son. Nobody knows."

"Why don't we go and have a look then, Father? If there's a dragon behind it, it will have been dead for ages anyway."

"Dragons never die, son."

"Hm!"

"You do as I tell you. Understood?"

The prince nodded and asked himself if by nodding you could be lying.

His mother the queen sobbed, her eyes wet with tears. "Please sweetheart, stay away from the cellar, then you won't be tempted. For if you go through the iv-ivory door, Mommy will never see you again and Mommy loves you so very much."

"Oh!" cried the prince. "May I have a chocolate then?"

She gave him ten if he promised not to go to the cellar.

He promised out loud while quietly not thinking about it, and he asked himself if by thinking quietly you could cancel out a lie.

Baroness Von Wetering Tetering threatened him with soap in his eyes. "If I see you going to the cellar, I'll rub soap into your eyes tonight. Then you won't be able to find that cursed door," she said.

"Ha ha, Minny!" cried the prince, and he danced round her, taking funny steps so that she had to laugh after all. Then he closed his eyes, stretched out his arms, and cried, "Blind! Blind! I'm a poor blind boy with soap in my eyes!" And he bumped into her, threw his arms round her waist, and pressed his head against her bosom because he loved her so.

"Gracious child!" she cried, but then she took his head in her hands and looked at him sternly. "Take care!" she said. "This isn't a game anymore, child. This is death."

But he laughed and shouted, "The dragon is dead and I'm going anyway," for he never lied to her. He raced through the long corridor, shouted "boo" in the dark alcoves, slid down the banisters, bumped down the stairs to the cellar, and looked for and found the side cellar where no one ever came but where the guard now stood with his fat tummy sticking out in front, and that is what the prince bumped into.

"Your Highness! Hm! Excuse me. You must not—"

"Is this the ivory door?"

"Yes, Your Highness."

"Is there a lion behind it? A dragon? A ghost? A demon? Have you heard any howling? Screaming? Crying?"

"Er, no, Your Highness."

The prince looked at the ivory door that shone a matte-white color in the light of two torches, and slowly his overconfidence subsided.

"Oh," he said. "Hm . . ."

The ivory door had been skillfully carved with horrifying monsters, the shadows of which moved in a lively manner in the sputtering light from the flames. The prince tried not to be impressed by it all. He bent forward to get a better look at the figures, but the guard held him back. "Er, Your Highness, er . . ."

But His Highness slipped past him. "It's locked, isn't it?" he cried. "With a steel key?" He rattled the handle. "You see? I can't get in there at all!" He put his ear to the door, rubbing against the hard heads of the monsters, but all he heard was the beating of his own heart. Bending over, he peeped through the keyhole, but all he could see was darkness.

"Your Highness! Your Highness!" The guard pulled at the prince's arm nervously. "I can't allow this."

"I won't tell anyone," said the prince. He pounded on the ivory with his fists and cried, "You just wait!" until the man dragged him away.

"I'll be back tomorrow!" cried the daredevil, and he ran up all the stairs, climbed on to the highest roof, and cried, "There's a dragon behind it! And a lion and a demon and a witch! I heard them howling!" And he slid down all the banisters in one go, ran into the garden, and plunged into the pond until he looked as black as a beetle.

The Baroness Von Wetering Tetering did not say anything when she sponged him in the bath that evening; she just looked at him with reproachful eyes. When she said good night, her voice sounded hoarse.

The prince could not sleep; he lay tossing and turning and when he closed his eyes, he saw the flickering light of the torches that shone on the ivory door and brought the carved figures to life. A horrifying lion with its mouth wide open, a snake with its head raised threateningly, a terrible crocodile—they snapped at him and caught hold of him and dragged him over the threshold of the door which was suddenly open and he fell into a black emptiness without walls and without a floor. He fell and fell and fell and woke up with a scream. And deep inside himself, he knew that it had not been a dream but a vision of the reality.

I'm never going there again, he thought.

And he didn't. Not for years. While he was growing up, the ivory door faded away in his thoughts, the fear faded away, the wariness faded away. A guard post was no longer necessary; the steel key was lying around somewhere. Prince Darrell had to study hard, and he sponged himself down in the bath in the evenings, but he was still called Prince Daredevil because now and again he still slid down the banisters or climbed on to the roof and cried "Hey, Minny!" when he saw Baroness Von Wetering Tetering sitting on the lawn. Then she wagged an angry finger at him laughingly and cried, "Gracious child!"

But one day his mother the queen became ill. She lay in her bed full of pink cushions, and the prince brought her a rose because she loved them so much.

"How tall you're growing," she said in a weak voice. "You're almost as tall as your father."

He looked at the portrait of his father that was hanging on the wall, and from there his gaze wandered to the cluttered table underneath it, littered with cups and glasses and tin dishes and rolls of parchment and a crumpled necktie and a pear and a rosary and a key.

A key! The steel key! It was as if a flashing spark flared up out of it and struck him in his soul. He jumped up, then restrained himself and walked slowly to the table, his heart beating, while he pretended that he wanted to look at the painting more closely.

"He was still young then, your father the king," said the sick queen from her bed.

"Yes," he answered hoarsely while his trembling hand took

the key from the table without her being able to see. "But he still looks like that," he added. Returning to her bed again, he kissed his mother good night with trembling lips. He walked to the door, but when he opened it, he bumped into Baroness Von Wetering Tetering, who was just about to go in. He was startled.

"Minny . . ." he said, "I . . ." The key burned in his hand. He held it behind his back, but she could hear that something was wrong by his hoarse voice and she could see by his attitude that he was hiding something.

"Gracious child!" She said it without laughing; she looked at him sternly and shook her head slowly.

He fled to his room and sat down panting. Why am I so jumpy? he thought. Why so excited? Why so furtive? The ivory door? Nothing but a trick from bygone days to scare little boys who are always touching everything. It is not even worth going to look. Oh, no? He thought further. You do not need to use a steel padlock for little daredevils, do you? And why put a guard post there? There must be something wrong with the door after all, he reasoned, and he argued from "go for it and expose the whole matter" to "don't do it, don't do it, death waits there." He imagined the skeletons of those who had gone through the ivory door in the past and who had died in a deep pit or in a never-ending labyrinth or in a swamp that sucks you down, and they were still lying there, their white bones in twisted postures. Or perhaps there was a nest of gluttonous ants over which you tripped in the dark and then you were attacked immediately by thousands of creepy-crawlies who gnawed over your whole body, feeling like thousands of pinpricks . . . Nonsense! He would not let himself get caught or get bogged down or drown or get gnawed on—he took a good lamp with him, filled with enough oil for three hours and with a fresh wick, and also took a torch, and then he went to have a look. Just a sensible, down-to-earth look.

He did it. He went. He went with the nerve of a daredevil who climbed onto roofs, slid down banisters, plunged into ponds, and called out "boo" in dark alcoves.

The Baroness Von Wetering Tetering woke up with a jolt. She had been dreaming—what had she been dreaming? Something nasty, something very—oh my God, her gracious child! She had dreamed that he stood in front of the ivory door with an oil lamp in one hand and a spluttering torch in the other. Half bent forward, he stood and looked at the ivory carving on the door and he was horrified by what he saw; the perspiration stood out on his forehead and his whole body trembled. And then he took the handle of the burning torch between his teeth, and with his free hand he pulled something out from under his clothes—a key! The steel key belonging to the door! Hesitantly he put it in the lock and turned it. It creaked.

Had she dreamed all that? Was she dreaming about it now? Or—

The baroness suppressed a shout, jumped out of bed, grabbed her night light, and ran, half groping, in the light of the faintly burning wick through the hall and down the stairs, her hair hanging loosely and the ties of her night attire flapping behind her. At the cellar door she saw the light, and as she plunged down the stone stairs she called out, "Gracious child! No! Don't do it!"

But the prince had already opened the ivory door. She could see that her dream was the reality. He stood there, half recoiling, staring into the black emptiness, but because of her approach, the daredevil in him got the upper hand. Activated by a feeling of "I'm going to do it anyway," he stepped across the threshold.

Boom! The bang made by the door closing behind him sounded fatal. The baroness, who threw herself against it, began to pound powerlessly on the ivory, her hands injured on the wide-open mouths of the monsters carved in it. "Child!" she sobbed. "Child, my child, my gracious child . . . !"

That same night, the news traveled through the castle like a terrible fire. The baroness woke the king, the sick queen heard it, the ladies-in-waiting, the cooks, the kitchen maids down to the lowliest servants and the youngest gardener, they all heard about it, and the youngest gardener ran to the inn in the village to tell them about it. The next morning, everyone knew about it: the young prince, Prince Daredevil, who was really called Darrell, has gone through the ivory door. Everyone understood what that meant: that they would never see him again. Never and never and never again.

Dreadful for the king. Dreadful for the queen. Dreadful for the baroness, for everyone at court, for everyone in the country, because Prince Daredevil was well loved. "He's lying at the bottom of the endless pit. Perishing to death," they said.

The same morning, all the flags were hanging at half mast and the castle was shrouded in black.

The prince had allowed the oil lamp to slip from his hand when the ivory door closed behind him. All that was left was the light from the torch, jumping against the drab stone walls—the beginning of an underground passage, which was swallowed up by a black hole. He stood motionless, the torch lifted up high, and he heard how the baroness's crying died away behind the door. Not a single sound got through to him anymore except the beating of his own heart. No shuffling or rattling or sighing or grumbling,

no creaking, nothing except the ringing in his own ears. It was as still as death there—only the threads of the cobwebs along the walls and on the ceilings moved in the draft and made creepy dancing shadow-figures.

Carefully, feeling with his foot, he took a step forward and another and another. Nothing changed, the black hole in front of him, the walls around him, the spluttering light in his hand; everything remained the same, with just as much uncertainty and lurking danger. Using his free hand, he felt the walls: cold stone, damp and hard. How old? How old? Who had built them and for what purpose?

He held the torch as far forward as possible, but the darkness in front of him did not let up for an instant. He took another ten careful steps: no change. A sandy floor, drab walls, whirling cobwebs, dead silence.

Should he shout? Make a noise?

No!

He tried to take another ten careful steps, but at the sixth step the wall on the left stopped altogether and became a black hole. A side passage? An alcove? The daredevil who had always shouted "boo" so bravely shrank back with fear and did not move an inch. Was someone waiting for him there? A big fellow? A ghost? A monster with a grasping claw that would pull him with it into the fathomless deep?

With his whole body trembling, he shuffled with one foot forward, crunching across the sand, and thrust his arm with the spluttering torch round the corner. When he finally dared to look, his faltering breath gave a squeak; there was no one to be seen. It was an alcove with a stone bench in it.

A bench! Had his predecessors sat on it? Kings of bygone days, princes, servants, his great-uncle, all those who had dared to take the dreadful steps through the ivory door and had never returned? Who had fallen into the bottomless pit further on and who still lay there, skeleton upon skeleton?

He walked up to the bench, touched the stone seat with his hand, wanted to lower himself onto it, but jerked up again at the thought that it was perhaps a trap. A bench that sank away as soon as the weight of a person was on it.

They will not catch me that easily, he thought suddenly, and the daredevil deep down inside him began to stir again. With a firmer pace he went on through the dark passage, and in the next alcove he shouted "Boo!" It made a terrifying echo that lasted a long time and only died away far in the distance. What was waiting for him there? A big man who kept dead quiet?

So what of it! He just went on walking and was very careful, waving to and fro with his torch so that all sides were well lit. It was better now; he walked on more resolutely. But torches do not burn indefinitely, he realized when the flame began to splutter more violently. How stupid, he thought, how stupid! I should have picked up the oil lamp and taken it with me. Then I could have lit it with this last bit of flame. Oh, how stupid!

He began to run steadily so that he could get as far as possible before total darkness surrounded him, but of course that was even more stupid—he could fall unexpectedly into the pit or the trap or the mouth or the pointed spear or the gluttonous ants or the barrel of acid or the swamp or the embrace of the black ghost ... and the last is what happened when the torch went out. It was so gloomy, so terribly dark, everything around him was absolutely black so that there was no difference between having his eyes open and having them closed. Even the air that he breathed was black and he groped around until he bumped against the wall so that he would at least have something to hold on to.

Step by step, he stumbled forward, ten paces, twenty, thirty, thirty-one—then he tripped over something on the floor and almost fell. He felt it, a pile of twigs? What lay there, what was it?

Bones! A skeleton! Heavens above! A skeleton that cracked when he stepped on it, belonging to one of the daredevils before him, a hundred years old or maybe two hundred. He had perished here. Yuck! And how had he perished?

He listened intently, held his breath . . . But he could not remain standing like that forever. He shuffled further carefully, lifting his feet up high, putting each foot down carefully to feel if the ground remained firm, his hand rubbing against the stone wall until suddenly it ended and he stood up in an emptiness. Another alcove? One yard before the ravine? Half a yard before a foot trap with razor-sharp spikes? Had the skeleton been in a trap? He had not even thought to examine it!

Suddenly he began to tremble uncontrollably. His whole body. Even his breath faltered, with soft squeaks like those of a distressed mouse. "Oh, God," he prayed. "Oh, God, why did I do this? Oh, God, rescue me."

But no one, that is what they had told him, had ever come back from here alive, had they? Not even dead . . .

I should have taken one of the bones with me, he thought, a piece of thigh bone from that skeleton. As a weapon. And to feel with on the ground, out in front of me and along the wall. Idiot!

Go back?

But he did not dare do that.

"Oh, God, rescue me from this," he prayed again. He felt behind him for the wall he had lost, took a step back and another, but could not find it anymore. With nothing to hold on to, with nothing to guide him, he stumbled on, feeling with his feet. He sank down onto his hands and knees so as to be able to feel more easily and to keep his balance, and he bumped his head against a rock.

"Ouch! Damn!"

It was a wall. Something to guide him. He crawled along it like a shy dog, his shoulders brushing against the rocks, stopping every now and then to listen. But he heard nothing, the black darkness was in his ears too, there was absolutely nothing.

Could it be, he thought suddenly, that there is absolutely nothing at all? That you just die of hunger and thirst here? Or that you die because of your own fear? Of nothing? Or did he hear a crackle there? Was he already near the ants' nest? Horrified, he crawled a little way back and listened intently. There was nothing to be heard. Were there no ants then, or were there ants which kept dead silent with their sharp jaws opened wide, all ten thousand of them ready to pounce on him?

He scraped a little sand from the floor and threw it in front of him. Nothing happened. He crept on, one hand in front of the other, one knee in front of the other, feeling, trembling, horrified, until he sank down and did not know or want anything anymore.

Does time go on in absolute darkness? Or does it stop? It is impossible to say how long Prince Darrell lay there, but the moment came when he opened his eyes and thought he saw a slightly less dark spot in the pitch darkness. Was there something there? Was there really a spot in the blackness that was less black? Or was his imagination playing tricks on him?

With great effort, he got himself up onto his hands and knees and crawled on. Until the moment actually came when he was sure that it was no imagination, that further on, a tiny bit of light was truly, really, actually appearing. A spot of light. To entice him? Were they standing there ready with knives and swords and red-hot pokers? Or . . .

He sniffed. The air smelled different, less musty; it brought back a memory of fresh air from outside—no, it could not be . . . But suddenly the prince could contain himself no longer. He crawled on like a maniac, faster and faster, and crawled to an upright position, ran further on both legs, shaking off all fear and danger, sniffing the fresh air, his eyes blinking in the light, and shouting, he dashed outside into the green leaves and twigs and branches and nettles and thorns and tough roots over which he tripped and fell flat on his face—thus he remained lying there panting, and perspiring with his nose in the soggy earth, and above his head the blue sky heralding a summer morning.

He was so relieved that he felt nothing of the scratches and bumps and grazes on his hands and face, and he certainly couldn't have cared less about the tears in his princely clothes. My God, he finally lay there thinking, what a sham! It is just an escape tunnel, an ordinary escape tunnel, a hundred years old. Or two hundred. Or three hundred. For escaping during a siege!

Slowly he began to free himself from the nettles and the brambles, the swaying twigs and the branches that caught on everything, beating off the horseflies and the wasps and ants and spiders. Wait! he thought. "Wait!" he shouted to the radiant summer morning, the waving grass, the chirping larks. "Wait! I'll show you something!"

And he cupped his hands round his mouth and shouted, "Here I am! I'm alive!!!"

"The prince is dead. Have you heard? Prince Daredevil. He's dead. He went through the ivory door."

Everyone had heard about it already. The whole country was in mourning, but work went on—the farmers have to go to their land early in the morning to milk their animals and later to lift the first potatoes. With leather patches on their knees, crawling along the sand, rooting in the soil, pulling up one lump after the other—"Hey there! Hey! Hey! You there! Peasants!" comes a sudden cry.

Who is that loudmouth? The farmers look up from their work: there on the path stands some tramp or other who is trying to imitate an upper-class accent. "What d'yer want?"

"What do I want?" comes the surprised answer. "Can't you see who I am?"

The farmers look at the tramp suspiciously and shake their heads. No.

"But, man! I'm the prince! Darrell! Prince Daredevil! I . . ."

The farmers turn toward each other, look at each other, get up slowly, threateningly. "What are you saying there?"

"I . . . I'm the prince, man! Look! That about the ivory —"

They do not let him finish. They push toward him. "Say that again if you dare!" One of the farmers gives him a push. "We don't like that kind of joke, young man! About one who's dead! Understand?"

The others pull him back. "Leave him, Krelis! The man's mad. He's just come from the madhouse. You can see that, can't you!"

"Mad?" cries Darrell. "Me, mad? I can't believe this. I'm —"

"Shut your big mouth and go to the devil. Go on, clear off!" They throw potatoes at him; one of them hits him painfully hard on the nose so that it pours with blood. With tears in his eyes, he runs away.

"He deserved it," says Krelis.

"He's a half-wit. Not right in his head."

"Sad all the same. Pretending to be the prince. Where would a half-wit like that get such an idea. In the midst of all this misery."

Darrell stumbles on, holding his nose between his thumb and his forefinger to stop it bleeding. In the distance, he can see the towers of his parents' castle sticking out above the trees. I shall clean myself up a little before I go home, he thinks. Silly of me not to realize that I look so disheveled.

Further on, there is an inn where he washes his hands and face, outside under the pump. His nose feels swollen, his clothes are full of tears and stains. He makes them look as respectable as possible, and then, full of expectation, he steps into the bar. "Good morning!" he cries loudly.

There is nobody there.

The landlady behind the bar teases him immediately by imitating his princely manner of speaking in an exaggerated upper-class tone. "Good morning, old chap!"

"Can't you see who I am?" he asks.

"Certainly," she says. " A highwayman acting like a clergyman."

He becomes red with anger. "But can't you see—"

"Oh, man!" she laughs. "Don't be such an idiot. Try and behave like a normal human being, that's bad enough."

"I . . . I . . . " He is nearly bursting. "But I'm the prince!" he says. "Prince Darrell, and I . . ."

"Oh, yes?" she says. "Well, then, I'm Queen Christina. Pleased to meet you!" She holds out her hand, red from all the scrubbing.

He shrinks back. "Don't you believe me?"

"Of course I do!" she cries. "Anyone can see that, can't they?"

He shrinks under her glance, which takes in his swollen nose, his tattered clothes, and the tear in his trousers. "A real prince, eh!" But then her eyes suddenly narrow. "Wait a minute," she says. "What did you say . . . Darrell? You mean Prince Daredevil? Prince Daredevil, who went through the ivory—" Her voice catches; she looks at him again carefully from top to toe, shakes her head slowly, and says, "You can't fool me, young man. I —"

"But I really am he!" he cries. "That story about the door is nonsense! Behind it, there's just a long passage. For escaping. It comes out among the bushes and that's why—"

"Yes, yes!" she cries, interrupting him. "Well thought out! When you heard about Prince Daredevil, you of course thought: I'll act as if I'm the prince, then I'll take his place. I'll make myself unrecognizably dirty, I'll bump my nose against something, I'll invent an underground passage—and from then on, I'll have a good life in the castle!"

Darrell has shrunk back further but is pushed forward again by a few men coming into the inn.

"Good mornin'!"

"Good mornin'!" cries the landlady in return. "Careful with him, please, he's the prince."

"Prince?" the men ask. They look at Darrell and turn their noses up.

"Yes, obviously," says one. "Just raised from the grave." They do not dare to laugh aloud now, but there is some sniggering going on and that makes the landlady angry. She does not want jokes made about one who is dead.

"That he's posing as him is bad enough," she says.

"But I am he!" Darrell begins, his voice breaking into a squeaky voice of indignation. "I am Darrell, damn it, and I . . . "

"Listen to him! He swears like a real prince too!" cries one of the men, and they all laugh aloud now.

The door opens again; more people come in with a buzzing of voices and a stamping of boots to shake off the sand. "It's unbelievable!" they are saying. "That they didn't stop him. It's unbelievable. They should've bricked it up a long time ago."

The landlady cries, "Are you talking about the prince? Shall I tell you something? There he is. There!" With a fat red sausage finger, she points at the disheveled stranger, who has retreated into a corner.

The men look. "That's no joke, Christina!"

"But he says that himself!" she cries back, and she imitates his dignified voice: "Damn it, man, I am Darrell!"

The men turn their heads in his direction again to look at him more carefully. "Looks just like him!" The sniggering starts again. "But it's sad all the same," they say, "very sad that idiots like that are walking about thinking they can deceive us all. Ugh! You clear off! Away with you! Off you go!"

The daredevil that was slinks away and slips outside through the door. Without looking up or around, he walks in the direction of the castle, in the direction of his parents' home. They know me there, he thinks to himself, and it is a reassuring thought. But is it so? Is it reassuring? Or can he feel the beginnings of confusion in his head? He shakes his head violently. No! No! I am not mad!

He walks and walks. The scratches on his arms and his face are smarting and the cold air penetrates through his thin trousers. It is only after some time that he notices he is being called again. "Pray with me!" calls the voice. "Pray with me for the repose of the prince!" Looking up, he sees a little church, and in the wide-open doorway someone is calling. "We are praying for the prince! His Highness went through the ivory door and came into the hands of the devil! Help us pray for his salvation!"

Darrell remains standing, his mouth opens wide, he wants to give up again, but the daredevil in him surfaces again irresistibly. "Yes, salvation!" he shouts and walks up to the man. "Exactly that! But you don't have to pray for it. It's already happened! I've been delivered. That story about the ivory door is nonsense! Do you hear me? Nonsense!" He pushes the man aside and roars into the little church between the mumbling people and through to the front and cries, "Stop it! Stop it! It's not necessary! Here I am, Prince Darrell! Safely back from the underground passage!"

"Ssh!" they hiss.

The priest stops praying, jumps up, grabs the disturber of the peace by his arm, and pushes him back between the people. But the prince keeps on shouting that he is the prince and that there is nothing behind the accursed ivory door, no dragon, no monster, no swamp, just an old escape passage which comes out somewhere among the nettles and that they should not be so silly as to disbelieve him, that they should not let themselves be misled by his appearance, that the nettles at the end of the tunnel had made him look like this, the nettles and the branches and twigs and the mean thorns and rotting leaves and foul turds covered in flies into which he had fallen and that there were absolutely no ants in the tunnel, only darkness, and that he had been afraid but as it turned out there was absolutely nothing, ha ha ha, not one dragon or ghost or spirit or devil —

In the midst of all this, at a wink from the priest, a couple of strong men drag the prince outside, half lifting him by the belt of his trousers, between the believers, who watch eagerly.

"But I am he!" he screamed with a cracking voice. "I am His Serene Highness Prince Darrell!"

"Lord!" prayed the priest, with a loud, imploring voice. "Deliver us from the devil!"

Thus the rumor spread that the devil had not only taken possession of the prince there behind the ivory door but that the devil was now walking about on earth pretending to be the prince.

It was not until they were quite a distance from the church that the men let him go with a final kick so that he fell with his painful nose even more painfully into a pool of mud. But even worse was the surge of fear that welled up in his soul: that of being totally lost. If no one knew him anymore, then he was no longer the person he had been, then he was no longer the prince, no longer the daredevil and no longer Darrell. No longer himself.

The pool of mud mirrored his face, bloodstained and soiled. "Who am I?" he asked himself, terrified. "Who am I? Who am I? Am I not who I am? Oh, my God . . ."

But then, with a shout, he raised himself and jumped up and with his daredevil voice he called, "We shall see!" And with a resolute step he walked straight to his father's castle.

The guards saw him coming from a distance. "Let me through!" they heard him cry. "Whether you believe me or not, I am the prince. I want to go to my parents!"

But they had received strict orders to stop irrevocably anyone who was posing as the prince, and that is what they did.

"But I am —"

"Yes, yes! That's what they all cry!"

"All?"

They gave no answer, just kept their spears pointed toward him.

He began to scream, to swear, and to rage with a high falsetto full of rage, powerlessness, fear, frantic fear of his own doubt, which penetrated his soul like poison.

"Please!" he begged. "Please get Minny. She'll recognize me. I know she will! Minny! Get Minny!"

"Minny?" they asked.

"Yes! My Baroness what's her name. Von Wetering Tetering. The Bar-Baroness Von —" His words became sobs. And he looked so lost and shabby and helpless that the younger guard began to melt and whispered to the other one, "We can do that, can't we?

For this poor creature. Warn the baroness. Then we'll see straight away . . ."

But the elder one said, "He's the devil. We've been specially warned about him, that he's the devil himself with all his arts of temptation. He's already started getting at you, I can see. If we get the baroness—if she'll come, then she'll fall for it too and —"

"Minny! Minny! Minny! Help me!"

"How could he know that the prince called her Minny?"

"The devil knows everything."

"Minny-y-y!"

The Baroness Von Wetering Tetering heard the call through the walls and the doors, and in stately indignation she came outside, forced her way past the guards, and stood right in front of him, her aristocratic head lifted high. "How dare you!" she said. "Her Majesty the Queen is seriously ill. The loss of her beloved son has shocked her terribly, and you have the coarse, atrocious cheek to pretend to be —"

"M-M-Minny . . . !"

"Get away! Child of the devil! Dreadful monster! Disappear!" Her angry outstretched arm showed him the way. Irrevocably.

And thus Prince Darrell who was called Prince Daredevil disappeared for good. Gone from his father's castle, gone from his parents, gone from his beloved baroness, and worst of all, gone from himself. He did not exist anymore. He had gone through the ivory door and—exactly according to the story—has never, never, never returned again.

Kit Pearson

The Eyes

I don't like her eyes," said Bernie. She pointed to one of the six dolls sitting on a shelf in her aunt's guest bedroom.

"That one?" said Aunt Sheila. She laughed. "I don't blame you. I never have either."

Michelle picked up the doll, straightened her green plaid skirt, and pushed her hair back under her bonnet. "What's wrong with her? She's pretty."

Bernie stared at the doll's face. Her porcelain cheeks were tinted with pink and her mouth curved into a half-smile. Michelle took her finger and rubbed dust out of the doll's eyes. They were a peculiar yellowy-orange, like a cat's eyes, veined with black and fringed all around with delicately painted lashes. The eyes seemed to be watching Bernie.

"She's very pretty," agreed Aunt Sheila. "The prettiest of all my childhood dolls. But I never played with her, partly because she's so fragile. That's why she's in such good condition." She put the doll back on the shelf. "You're both welcome to play with any of these, though."

Bernie looked longingly at the other five dolls, but Michelle said, "We're too old for dolls."

"Shall I leave the hall light on for you?" Aunt Sheila asked.

"No thanks," said Michelle. "Bernie and I *like* the dark, right?"

"Uh huh," gulped Bernie.

"Good night then, girls. Sleep as long as you want in the morning. I'm so glad to have you here at last." Aunt Sheila kissed them both and went downstairs.

Michelle was silent almost immediately, but Bernie couldn't sink into the sleep her exhausted body craved. It had been such a long day, flying clear across Canada to this large city on the west coast.

She and Michelle were spending the last three weeks of the summer vacation with Aunt Sheila, their father's sister. They saw her every Christmas in Nova Scotia when she visited her parents. She was their favorite aunt, and she had been so excited when Bernie and Michelle had finally accepted her yearly invitation to visit.

They hadn't come before because of Bernie. She was afraid of flying, even with her older sister along. And Michelle wasn't allowed to go alone—their parents said it wasn't fair. "You're such a coward!" she hissed at Bernie every year she'd refused.

This year Dad had sat Bernie down after her tenth birthday and thought he'd persuaded her to do it. But it was Michelle's disdain that Bernie couldn't stand any longer.

Michelle was only a year older than Bernie, but she was trying to grow up as fast as she could. She had all sorts of standards. Saying "Dad" instead of "Daddy"; not playing with dolls after age eight; getting your ears pierced at ten. Bernie had been relieved when their parents extended this to twelve; *she* didn't want holes poked in her ears.

Bernie tried her best to live up to her sister's expectations, but she was afraid of so many things that it was often difficult. The plane trip had been awful. Her body was still taut with the fear she'd struggled with the whole time. It didn't matter how kind the flight attendant was or how nice Michelle was to her on the plane. She couldn't eat, and when they arrived her legs wouldn't work properly.

"See?" said Michelle as they walked into the airport. "I told you it would be easy."

Only Aunt Sheila understood. "Was it terrible, poor Bernie?" she whispered through her hug. "I'm so proud of you. It's very brave to make yourself do something that frightens you so much."

And now here they were, safely in Aunt Sheila's house in Vancouver. It was close to the beach and they were going there first thing tomorrow. Aunt Sheila had taken time off work and she had lots of treats planned for them—a trip to Victoria on the ferry, to a water park, to movies and the rides at the exhibition. And in the third week Mom and Dad were flying out to join them.

Bernie hunched further under the quilt. She should be ready to sleep off her ordeal. So why was she still so tense?

Because the room was so dark; at home the hall light *was* left on.

It was silly to feel scared. If she'd conquered the plane, she should be able to face the dark. She pulled the quilt from her face and turned over on her back.

High on the shelf opposite the bed, the doll's eyes glittered— two yellow orbs in the blackness, staring straight at Bernie.

Bernie shrieked, but no sound came. She hid her head, then glanced out again. The eyes still shone and their pupils swelled and shrank like those in real eyes.

"Michelle!" squealed Bernie, leaping to her sister's bed and shaking her.

Michelle thrashed and groaned. "Leave me *alone*, I'm asleep!"

"Michelle, p-please . . . " Bernie crawled into bed beside her sister and whispered into her ear. "That d-doll—her eyes are— they're alive! They're shining! Look!"

"You are such an idiot . . . " Michelle sat up briefly, glanced at the doll, and flopped down. "They are *not*, Bernie. Get back into your own bed and let me sleep!"

Bernie made herself look again. "They *are!*"

But Michelle pushed Bernie onto the floor, turned her back to her, and didn't move.

Bernie jumped back under her own covers. She curled up in the hot cave, breathing hard.

Was she dreaming? She risked one more peek, then dived under again. The flickering eyes were even brighter. They burned into Bernie's own eyes.

Bernie clutched her knees to her chest and stayed that way until her body finally collapsed into sleep.

"Weren't you hot, sleeping under the covers all night?"

Bernie's head emerged. Michelle was her usual zealous morning self. She rushed to the window. "It's a great day for the beach! Let's put our bathing suits on under our shorts."

But Bernie stayed in bed, rigidly not looking at the shelf.

"Bernie? What's the matter, are you sick?"

"That doll," whispered Bernie. "She was staring at me all night. I could feel her eyes, even though I hid under the quilt. I could feel her staring even when I was asleep."

Michelle was pulling off her pajamas. "Honestly, Bernie. It was a *dream.* You were probably dreaming about that video we rented about a doll that came alive."

"I didn't watch that," said Bernie, shuddering.

"Well, it must have been a dream. She's just a doll—look and you'll see."

Taking a deep breath, Bernie sat up and turned her head toward the doll.

Michelle was right—she was just a doll. She gazed blankly into the air the way the other dolls did, not at Bernie. Her yellow eyes glinted a bit in the sunlight, but they were just glass, not alive.

"Maybe it *was* a dream," said Bernie slowly.

"Of course it was. Come on, let's go wake up Aunt Sheila."

That night Bernie considered asking Aunt Sheila to put the doll somewhere else. But now that she felt relaxed she was more and more convinced that the gleaming eyes had been only a dream.

They'd had a wonderful day. The Pacific Ocean was much warmer than the Atlantic. They had swum and made castles with moats that filled up when the tide came in. They had lunch at a hamburger stand and went to Stanley Park in the afternoon.

Bernie and Michelle lay in bed and chatted drowsily until Michelle's last sentence dwindled away. Bernie fell asleep soon after.

A few hours later she shuddered violently, turned over, and woke up. Someone was looking at her. She *knew* it. Whoever it was compelled her to open her eyes and look back.

The amber eyes floated in the darkness as if they weren't connected to a face. They seemed even more full of menace than last night.

Bernie stumbled out of the room and down the stairs. She crawled into bed with Aunt Sheila.

"What's the matter, Bernie? You're shaking!"

"The eyes—the *eyes* . . . " sobbed Bernie.

Aunt Sheila drew her close and tucked her blanket around both of them. "It's all right, sweetheart. You've had a nightmare. Go back to sleep—you're safe now."

"Aunt Sheila, please take that doll out of our room," said Bernie at breakfast.

"What a baby!" scoffed Michelle. "Do you still think it's looking at you?"

"Yes," whispered Bernie.

"Leave her alone, Michelle." Aunt Sheila patted Bernie's shoulder. "If the doll bothers you, of course I'll take it away."

Bernie wouldn't go into the bedroom until Aunt Sheila carried the doll down to the basement. She watched from the top of the stairs as her aunt wrapped the doll in an old towel, put her into a cardboard box, and closed the flaps.

"There!" Aunt Sheila looked up at Bernie. "She can stay in this box until you leave, all right?"

Bernie wasn't sure if it was all right. The doll was out of sight, but her fiery eyes were still in Bernie's mind.

She tried to think of other things. Their cousin Jennifer came over, and Bernie and Michelle were surprised that Jennifer, at thirteen, suggested playing with Aunt Sheila's dolls.

"Of course I'm too old for this," she said, taking a tiny leather boot out of the bag of dolls' clothes. "But isn't it neat how Aunt Sheila has kept these? I've played with them all my life. But where's the other one—the fancy one with the china face?"

Please don't tell her, Bernie begged Michelle silently.

Luckily Michelle didn't seem to want to admit that her sister was a coward. "What other one?" she asked innocently.

"There's one more doll. Maybe Aunt Sheila put her away so you wouldn't break her. She has a funny name—Grizel!"

Michelle giggled. "Grizel?"

"Isn't it weird? She came from Scotland—she belonged to our great-grandmother, the one who came to Canada with her husband." Jennifer finished tying the tiny boot laces and looked up. "Do you want to see her?"

"See who?" whispered Bernie.

"Grizel! I'm sure Aunt Sheila would show her to you."

Michelle looked at Bernie. "No, thanks. Bernie and I are too old for dolls. Come on, it must be time to go to the movie."

Bernie tried to lose herself in the movie, but she couldn't help thinking of Grizel. Now that she knew her name, the doll felt even more alive. It suited her—an ugly name for something ugly that stared out of the doll's pretty face.

She remembered what Dad had said when he talked to her about flying. "If you're scared of something, find out more about it." He had shown her statistics about how safe flying was.

It hadn't helped—Bernie had still spent the whole time thinking the plane was going to crash. But maybe it would help with Grizel. She had to do something to get the image of the doll's burning eyes out of her head.

That evening she helped her aunt load the dishwasher while Michelle and Jennifer watched TV. "Aunt Sheila," she began carefully, "could you tell me more about that doll I don't like? Jennifer said her name was Grizel and that she belonged to our great-grandmother."

"I . . . suppose I could. First let me make some tea."

Bernie watched her aunt pour water into the teapot and get out the cups. She poured Bernie tea with lots of milk in it, and they sat down at the kitchen table.

Why did Aunt Sheila seem so reluctant to speak? "It's okay," said Bernie. "I don't really want to know any more about the doll."

Aunt Sheila stirred her tea. "No, I'm glad you asked. You girls *should* know, Bernie. Maybe you especially."

"Why?"

"Because you're so imaginative and sensitive. Like Grizel's owner—your great-grandmother Margaret. You even look a bit like her."

"Did you ever meet her?"

Aunt Sheila nodded. "I knew her all my childhood, although no one knew her well. She was a very reserved woman and she always looked sad. But one day toward the end of her life she told me a tragic story. I was only sixteen, but I've never forgotten it." Aunt Sheila put a hand on top of Bernie's. "Shall I tell you? I don't want to give you nightmares again."

Bernie swallowed hard. "Tell me."

"It was about a fire," Aunt Sheila began slowly. Bernie's insides quaked. One of her nighttime fears was of a fire occurring while she was asleep.

"Grannie grew up on the east coast of Scotland. She had two older sisters and a younger brother—his name was Ewan, and she adored him. She used to pull him around the town streets in a wagon, and they shared a room. The other thing she adored was her doll."

"Grizel," breathed Bernie.

"Yes—a funny name to us but a common one in Scotland then. It's a nickname for Grizelda. Margaret was given Grizel for her eighth birthday, and she took her everywhere for the next four years. Girls grew up more slowly then—it wasn't unusual for a twelve-year-old to play with dolls. Margaret and Ewan constantly made up stories about Grizel—how she was really a princess and lived in a land called . . . Ilore or something. I know—Eleuria."

Bernie smiled; sometimes when she couldn't sleep, she made up an imaginary land. "Did she tell you much about Eleuria?"

"Not really—she was a bit embarrassed about it, but it was obvious she remembered a lot of what they pretended. She said that she and Ewan talked about Eleuria all the time. They used to carry Grizel around on a red cushion, and Margaret sewed royal clothes for her."

Bernie thought of Grizel's terrifying eyes—obviously they hadn't bothered these two long-ago children.

"One evening Margaret's parents and older sisters went to a lecture. They left Margaret in charge of Ewan. She was twelve and he was six. They trusted her to take good care of the brother she loved so much. They weren't going to be late."

Aunt Sheila sighed, took a deep drink of tea, and continued. "They didn't have electricity in their house—they used paraffin lamps. Margaret and Ewan propped up Grizel on a high shelf and pretended to be courtiers bringing her presents. They draped themselves in shawls and began dancing for Grizel. Then Margaret had to go to the outside toilet. She said Ewan was still whirling around when she left. The edge of his shawl must have knocked over a lamp. Margaret heard him scream and ran back into the house, but she was overcome by smoke and fainted outside the room."

Bernie gasped, and Aunt Sheila put an arm around her shoulder as she continued. "Her family arrived home just in time to drag her to safety. But it was too late for Ewan—he was burned to death."

Neither of them spoke for a minute. Finally Bernie whispered, "What about Grizel?"

"Grannie said she wasn't damaged at all. When the fire brigade arrived she got soaked with water and she smelled of smoke for months afterward—but she was sitting up so high she escaped the flames."

Aunt Sheila sighed. "I don't think Grannie ever got over it. She blamed herself for Ewan's death—that's why she always looked so sad."

She paused, looking sad herself.

"There's more, isn't there?" whispered Bernie.

"Yes . . . Grannie said that from then on Grizel changed. That her eyes turned from gray to yellow. And that sometimes, in the dark—"

"They gleamed," whispered Bernie. "I saw them, Aunt Sheila. They shone in the dark, and they moved—like real eyes."

"That's exactly what Grannie said. She told me it terrified her so much she wanted to give Grizel away. She began to hate Grizel, but she had to keep her—she was the last person to see Ewan alive, you see."

"Did you ever see her eyes shine like that?" Bernie asked. "Did your mother?"

"Never." Aunt Sheila pushed back her chair. "There are lots of things you can't explain. I think I'll shut up Grizel in that box from now on. Grannie made me promise never to give her away, so I have to keep her, even though she gives me the creeps—I just won't let her out." She laughed. "Listen to me, I'm talking as if she's real."

"Her eyes are," whispered Bernie.

"That's so hard to believe," said Aunt Sheila gently. "Sometimes I think that it's just your—and Grannie's—overactive imagination. But I'm a much more down-to-earth person than you are. Michelle's like me—but you're different. Maybe you see things that we can't."

She hugged Bernie. "Let's go and join the others and forget about Grizel. Can you try to stop thinking about her?"

Bernie nodded, but she knew it was impossible.

For the rest of the week, as Bernie traveled around the city with her sister and aunt, Grizel's feverish eyes glittered inside her brain. They seemed to be asking something of her.

Finally Bernie gave in. One afternoon, when Aunt Sheila had

taken Michelle to get her hair cut, Bernie crept down to the basement.

She carried the cardboard box upstairs so she wouldn't have to open it in the dark. Placing it on the table in the sunny kitchen, Bernie pried open the flaps and unwrapped the towel.

Grizel looked ordinary again—at least, as ordinary as she could with those eerie eyes. But they just reflected the light like any glass eyes.

Bernie lifted out the doll and examined her. She *was* beautiful—no wonder Margaret and Ewan had pretended she was a princess. Grizel's dark hair was as soft as real hair and her long fingers were so carefully modeled.

But Bernie remembered how Grizel's eyes looked in the darkness. She started to put the doll back into the box. But as she closed the flaps the golden eyes seemed to implore her.

Bernie took her out again and held her on her lap, careful not to bang her porcelain arms and legs together. The middle part of Grizel was made of cloth, stuffed with something firm; she made a nice weight.

It wasn't Grizel's fault that her eyes reflected such horror. It was because of what she had *seen*, what she had witnessed as she sat trapped on the shelf in the room full of flames. And she hadn't been able to close her eyes, like a human could. A doll had to keep looking.

Bernie shivered and held Grizel closer. Margaret had come to hate her, Aunt Sheila said—as if Grizel represented Ewan's suffering. What a lot to bear—she was only a doll!

Only a doll . . . Bernie hugged Grizel harder as she made up her mind.

What if she began to *play* with Grizel, as her former owners had played with her? Dolls weren't meant to be hated—they were meant to be taken care of, to be dressed and groomed and talked to. Maybe Grizel could become a real doll again—maybe her eyes would even forget what they had witnessed.

I can do it as long as it's daytime, decided Bernie. She could shut Grizel into the box every night. But in the daytime—right now!—she could treat Grizel like an ordinary doll.

Aunt Sheila and Michelle were surprised to find Bernie sitting in the kitchen and doing what everyone does with a doll—fixing her hair.

Now Grizel was with Bernie every moment before bedtime. Bernie combed and braided her hair and tied it with ribbons. She sorted out all the clothes from the other dolls that would fit Grizel and changed her outfit every day. She found some shiny material in Aunt Sheila's sewing box and sewed Grizel a cape. With her allowance she went to a craft store and bought sequins for the cape and fake rhinestones that she glued onto a cardboard crown.

"Princess Grizel," Bernie called her. She made necklaces for her out of a bead kit and yearned for a toy horse on wheels she had at home. It would be just the right size for Grizel to ride on.

Bernie took Grizel everywhere she went, even to Victoria on the ferry.

"You're too old to play with dolls," said Michelle.

"No, I'm not," said Bernie, surprising herself with her confidence. "Aunt Sheila said our great-grandmother played with dolls when she was twelve. And Jennifer likes her."

It was true. Jennifer came over almost every day, and she began to help Bernie make things for Grizel. By the end of the week even Michelle was giving them ideas for their map of Eleuria. Aunt Sheila became involved too. They spent evenings making up names for the members of the royal household. Aunt

Sheila said they could paint her old doll's bed so that it was fit for a princess. It rained for three days straight, but none of them cared—they were immersed in an enchanted world that revolved around Princess Grizel.

Only at night was Grizel banished. At first Bernie left her in the box in the kitchen. Then she took the box up to her room, so Grizel would at least be near. But she always closed the flaps.

"Your parents are arriving on Sunday," Aunt Sheila reminded them one afternoon.

"Already?" said Michelle.

They were sitting on the deck making papier-mâché dishes for Grizel. When they were dry they would paint them gold.

But now Michelle put down her dish as if it repulsed her. "This is so boring," she said. "Can't we go to the mall, Aunt Sheila? I'd like to buy that ring I saw so I can show it to Mom."

"I suppose so." Aunt Sheila added more paste to her bowl. "Want to come, Bernie?"

Bernie pretended not to hear. It was as if a spell had been broken. She picked up Grizel and retied the bow on her cape. "There," she said. "Now you're ready to receive the ambassador of Eleuria." But Michelle and Aunt Sheila and Jennifer were already getting ready to go.

"Mom and Dad are going to be surprised you're playing with dolls," said Michelle that evening.

"I don't care. Anyway, you played with her too."

Michelle reddened. "I wasn't really playing. I was just going along with you because there was nothing else to do. I think you're acting really strange about that doll, Bernie. She's only a doll—you're obsessed with her."

"I know she's only a doll," said Bernie. "It's just a game, but I like it. I *like* pretending things."

Michelle shrugged. "Suit yourself." She got into bed.

Bernie was pleased. She'd said what she thought and Michelle accepted it. Could it be that easy? Could she simply refuse to go along with Michelle if she didn't want to?

I can do what I want! she thought in wonder. For the past week she had, and she'd been so successful that she'd enticed Michelle and Jennifer and even Aunt Sheila into her game. She'd thought it was Grizel that had put a spell over them, but it was *her*, Bernie . . .

She gazed at Grizel as she put her in her box for the night. She was only a doll. Only a human, like herself, could make her seem real.

Bernie looked at her and saw—but she knew it was her imagination that saw—how lonely Grizel looked. Despite being groomed and taken on outings and dressed and worshipped and imagined in all sorts of stories about Eleuria, she didn't like going into exile every night. Imagine a princess being shut into a cardboard box!

Bernie took her out and tucked her into the bed she'd painted. But even there Grizel's amber eyes yearned.

What did dolls like? To sleep beside their owners, of course. To be cuddled in a nice warm bed and whispered to in the dark. That's what Bernie had done with the dolls she used to play with.

But the eyes . . .

Her eyes were like that because my great-grandmother hated her, thought Bernie. Now someone loves her—I do. Now she's a real doll again, with eyes that are ordinary glass.

Despite her beating heart, she undid Grizel's cape, took off her dress, and put one of the other dolls' nightgowns on her.

When Aunt Sheila came up to kiss them good night Grizel was tucked up beside Bernie.

"Good for you," said Aunt Sheila, smiling. "You're not afraid of her at all anymore, are you? Just be careful not to roll on her."

"Imagine still sleeping with a doll," scoffed Michelle, but Bernie just turned her back and hugged Grizel.

She caught a faint whiff of smoke—but surely that was her imagination. "Go to sleep," she whispered.

Bernie turned over and felt one of Grizel's stiff arms jab her side. She woke up at once—had she lain on the doll's arm and broken it? She picked up Grizel and felt her arm in the darkness.

The eyes—they glittered and blazed and seethed with fire. Bernie gasped and dropped Grizel on the quilt.

But some new strength made her pick up the doll again. Something made herself clutch Grizel and stare into her eyes.

The eyes danced with leaping flames. The eyes crackled with fright and shock and horror. Bernie's whole body shook as she saw what Grizel saw.

Flames licking at a little boy's clothes and then at the flesh of his face and hands. Screams that turned to chokes and then silence as the small body gave in to the fierce heat of the fire. Smell of scorched clothes and something far worse—scorched flesh.

Bernie hung on to the doll. She wanted to close her eyes but she couldn't—because Grizel hadn't been able to. She was caught in the doll's witnessing of a senseless, monstrous accident. Part of her wanted to fling the horror away, to throw Grizel out of her bed, but she continued to clutch her and watch, too appalled to utter a sound.

And then she knew something else—she knew that Margaret had witnessed the fire as well. That she *had* been able to get into the room but had been too terrified to do anything. That she'd stood, paralyzed with fright, and watched her brother burn to death—and then she had turned to run for help and fainted outside the door.

Margaret had seen what no one should have to see, and she had never told anyone. She'd held that horror inside her for the rest of her life. That was why she hated Grizel yet couldn't give her away. She kept the doll to torment herself with her guilt.

Finally it was over. The flames died out in the eyes and they became as dim as the rest of the doll's features. Bernie pulled Grizel close to her. "It's not your fault," she whispered. "You couldn't help it. You would have been burned yourself if you'd gone to him. There was nothing you could do."

She fell asleep cradling Grizel and Margaret.

"Where did you get that beautiful doll?" asked Mom, after all the exclamations and hugs and kisses were over and they were waiting for the luggage to appear.

Grizel had worn her best cape for going to the airport. "She was Aunt Sheila's—but she just told me I could have her!" said Bernie proudly.

Mom held Grizel. "What gorgeous gray eyes—they look right at you, don't they?"

"Gray?" said Michelle.

"Let me see." Aunt Sheila took Grizel. "Why, look—her eyes aren't yellow anymore!"

"Weird," said Michelle. "Did you paint them or something, Bernie?"

Bernie just smiled as she claimed Grizel back. "Her eyes were always this color," she said softly. "You just didn't look at them the right way."

Bjarne Reuter

Grandfather's Clock

Bright summer weather. Otto is standing in his grandfather's overgrown garden looking at the chestnut tree. Suddenly the sky opens. Just like a flower. Otto would like to call his father so that he too can see what is happening on this bright day when a rope comes down from the sky. A long, twisted rope, one that is used to tie up ships by the quayside. It twists down until it is hanging right in front of Otto. It is an unbelievable sight. It is only now that Otto sees his grandfather. He is holding the other end of the rope with his hands.

"Noa," says Grandfather. "Noa, my boy." Otto's grandfather always calls him Noa. "Get hold of the rope, Noa."

Otto grasps the rope. It cuts into the palms of his hands as if there are glass splinters in it. "My hands," cries Otto. "It hurts my hands, Grandfather. They're bleeding. I can't. I'm sorry, I can't. I'm sorry."

He cries as loudly as he can. He is in a cold sweat.

"Otto! Otto, wake up. Can you hear me?"

Otto can see his mother sitting on the edge of his bed. The light is burning in the hall.

"You're all wet, son." She holds him tight. Otto's father comes in too. He looks sleepy and asks what time it is. "Half past three," says Otto's mother.

"Did you have a nightmare, Otto?" his mother asks him.

Otto nods, still a little confused. He looks at his father, who asks if it was about his grandfather again. Mother still holds Otto tight, but Otto pulls himself free, lays back down, and pulls the covers up. His parents leave him then, closing his door behind them. On the other side of the wall, he can hear his mother saying that it is beginning to get unhealthy and that now he should really accept that dead is dead. Dead and done with. His father says that he is tired and doesn't want to talk about it now.

Every day they pack things up. All three of them pack, but his parents in particular. Otto hates clutter. The worst kind of clutter he can imagine is a moving box crammed full with his things. An empty apartment. There is nothing wrong with the house they are going to. It is big and beautiful and they will have twice as much space. And a garden. "You can plant your own chestnut tree there, Otto," his father had said.

In the dining room there are five big trash bags. His parents fill them until they are absolutely full. Otto hates throwing things away. One night he got up to look through the bags, to make sure they had not thrown away anything he definitely wanted to keep.

He gets up again and goes and sits on the windowsill. It is almost light. He likes sitting on the windowsill, watching it getting light. That is to say, you cannot actually see it. Sometimes when he stayed with his grandfather they got up early to watch it getting light.

"It's a wonder, every time again," his grandfather had said, coughing at the same time.

Otto crept to the room where the longcase clock was. It had not worked for ages. They had inherited it the previous year when Grandfather died, but they had never found the key to wind it up. Otto crept into his father's study and pulled a drawer open. In the drawer, there lay a stamp album, a magnifying glass, a photo of his grandfather in his younger years, and a box of cigars. Old, dry, mud-brown-colored cigars, the Caminande brand. Twelve altogether. Grandfather had smoked the rest. When he was still alive. Otto liked smelling the cigars. To close his eyes and take a deep breath. Then the image of Grandfather appeared immediately. Surrounded by the soft, dry, brown smell. It smelled like a hand. Big and warm, rough and yet soft.

"Otto!"

He shrank back. His father was on his way to the bathroom. No, not now, thought Otto.

His father came into the study, locked the cigar box, and put it back into the drawer. He told Otto to crawl back into bed, on the double.

"Those confounded cigars are certainly not going to move with us, Otto."

"Dad . . ."

"Sleep well, Otto. We've already had that discussion. The cigars are going!"

"You mustn't throw them away. Promise me you won't throw them away!"

"I said good night, Otto."

His father went to the bathroom. Otto could hear the splashing noise and waited patiently until he had finished.

"Are you still here?" grumbled his father.

"How did it happen?"

"How did what happen, Otto? Are you aware of the fact that it's the middle of the night and that I—"

"How did it happen exactly, with Grandfather at the shipyard?"

"For goodness sake, Otto." His father pushed Otto back into his room and into bed.

"You've always said that he fell over and then he was dead. But I heard Mommy saying that perhaps it wouldn't have happened if he'd been wearing a helmet. I think you just say any old thing."

"I never just say any old thing. Good night, Otto."

"Why aren't we allowed to talk about it?"

"Of course we're allowed to talk about it. Grandfather's dead."

"Something fell on his head."

"Okay then, something fell on his head. That kind of accident happens at a shipyard. Are you satisfied now?"

"What fell on his head?"

Daddy went to his bedroom and shut the door behind him.

Otto looked at the door and repeated the question to himself. The smell of the dry cigars still hung in his nose. It evoked a yellowed image. One beautiful summer's day: Otto and his grandfather are sitting on the terrace. Grandfather is polishing the weights belonging to the longcase clock. The smoke from his cigar gets in his eyes all the time. That is why he is wearing his welding goggles. "When I'm not here anymore, you'll get this old clock, Noa," he says as he hooks the weight on again and turns the small hand. He smiles at Otto.

They listen to the frail melody that resounds from the clock. It is as if it has something to say to them. Only them. Perhaps it tells a story about what they have together, a story without words, just a tiny, tinkling melody. Afterward, they carry the clock into Grandfather's room. It is heavy. Only when it is standing in place does Otto look at the palms of his hands, where drops of blood are appearing from tiny cuts. Grandfather fetches a bottle of iodine.

"Are you all right now, Noa?"

"Yes, thank you, fine."

He took a roundabout route on his way home from school. Kept an eye on the sky, which looked as if it were made of lead. The

houses looked like pieces of coal. A strange day. He took his sweater off. The air was warmish. A little later, he was standing in the clockmaker's shop. The note lay on the counter. On it, he had written the name that was on the clock: Anton Kehl, 1898.

Otto asked the clockmaker if he could make a new key. He knew his parents had said that it was impossible because the clock was too old and too rare.

"Everything's possible," said the old clockmaker, "if you're willing to pay enough money. But a key for a Kehl clock has to be made by hand. That's impossibly expensive."

"The clock used to play a song at six o'clock and at twelve o'clock."

The clockmaker said he knew that.

It had started to rain outside. Big, soft raindrops beat against the shop window. When Otto opened the door to the shop, a flash of lightning shot across the sky. Just for a moment, there was a gigantic claw of blue neon light in the sky. Then it disappeared again. Otto looked at his watch. It was late.

"Are you in a hurry, Noa?"

The woman was leaning against the wall of the house. She smiled at Otto and took off her old-fashioned brown beret. Otto looked at her clothes, her short jacket and her wool trousers. She was wearing sunglasses, round glasses with thick rims. They looked almost like welding goggles. Or was she in fact a man?

"Do we know each other?" Otto used his hand to shield his eyes against the sudden sun. She was white without being pale. Only her lips had color. A color that was alive. Otto had a distinct feeling that he had met this man before. But he could not think where or when.

He walked on. He did not really like being accosted like that. When he came to the first corner, he looked over his shoulder to see if the other person was following him. She was not. Or he. Or whatever it was. She had disappeared. Otto shook his head and crossed over. The sun was shining again now. The greengrocer was shaking the water from his awning and at the cafe on the corner, chairs were being put out again.

Otto stood still. He suddenly felt very strange. Empty. As if he were leaking. Slowly he walked back along the houses, past the clockmaker's, where he stood still for a moment and looked round. The stranger had said Noa. And there was only one person in the whole world who had ever called him Noa.

"What's this, are you ill?"

Otto turned over so that he was lying on his back and looked at his mother.

"No, I'm just resting."

"You, resting?"

"Yes, that's what I said, wasn't it?"

"Why don't you go and pack up a few of your things? You've hardly done anything. Actually, I also wanted to ask if you'd mind going to buy some rice and a few leeks. Will you do that?"

Otto swung his legs over the edge of the bed and took the money. His mother felt his forehead.

Otto repeated, rather irritated, that he was not ill. He liked walking round the supermarket. It was nice seeing people and watching what they bought. He went straight to the rice and the vegetable sections.

"Your name's Noa, isn't it?"

He stiffened. He recognized the voice immediately, without having to turn round. Noticed straight away how he got that empty feeling. The man or the woman, he still had no idea which, was engrossed in the tobacco section.

"How do you know my name? For that matter, I'm not called Noa at all."

"Oh, I'm sorry. What should I call you, then?"

Otto stared up at the other person, in whose sunglasses he could see only himself. "Do we know each other?"

"I believe we've met before. In a workshop."

Otto decided it was a woman. He could not concentrate if he had to keep asking himself if it was a man or a woman.

"I don't think I've ever been in a workshop," Otto said softly.

"We made figures out of chestnuts and matches."

"You're dotty."

Otto walked backwards, slowly at first and then more quickly.

He walked hurriedly between the shelves with groceries to the cash registers, where he threw his bag of rice and the leeks onto the moving belt. As he was looking for his money, he glanced behind for the stranger. But obviously she had gone again.

The change rolled into the small metal bowl. Otto looked at the cashier's mouth, which was moving. His fingers held tight onto the rail next to him. Chestnut figures. Suddenly he had a strong urge to cry. Animals with wobbly legs made of matches.

Under the tree lies the fruit with the spiky skin. Grandfather is standing on it to break it open—not too hard and not too soft. They sit together on the bench all day long making chestnut animals, giraffes, monkeys, bears, and cows. In the smoke from Grandfather's cigar. In the sun which sets slowly. That summer. That beautiful summer. Grandfather's last one. The last one for him and for Otto.

Ellinor came after dinner. That surprised Otto, even though the arrangement was that she would come every Thursday evening. She was in the same class as Otto and they shared one passion. Chess. Usually they played timed games, but not always. Tonight they did not. Ellinor was just twelve. She had been a punk since she was nine. With three rings in her nose, two in her ears, short green hair, and big black boots. In addition to that, she was a terrible giggler and a treacherous chessplayer. Especially in the endgame.

After five moves, Otto said, "Are there any people who are neither man nor woman?"

"Except for our math teacher, I've never met one. Bishop to . . ."

"Ellinor, I can't concentrate this evening. Sorry." Otto went and sat on the windowsill.

"If I had to move, I'd have jumped on a truck long ago."

"It's not that. In fact, I've gotten used to the idea. It's something different."

Ellinor said that adolescence was very much underestimated as a factor for causing stress. Otto thought how he would miss her when they had moved. He looked straight at her and said, "I'm being followed by some idiot or other, who talks to me as if we know each other. It's driving me mad."

Sensibly, Ellinor asked if it could be a pervert. Otto did not know exactly what she meant but suggested that they go for a walk.

It was lovely weather. Otto and Ellinor walked on opposite sides of the road so no one would think they were a couple. They always chose a route where there were narrow streets so that they could shout to each other. Ellinor was shouting over about a Sicilian opening move and about Kasparov's latest match when Otto stopped and stood still under a white lilac tree. The perfume from the flowers made him smile.

"My grandfather always fell asleep when he smelled this kind of flower," he said. "At least, in the month of June. A vase of lilac stood on his bedside table then."

"Are you still talking about that grandfather of yours?"

Ellinor went on talking about the one time she had offered to bring the chess match to a tie without it even being really necessary. Otto looked at her. It was not easy for her with those boots on, maybe because she took such big strides.

"Do you want to see him again?"

Otto turned round. His breathing changed so that it became dangerously rapid. Where did the voice come from? He did not need to ask whose voice it was because he knew.

"Are you talking to me? Why didn't you say so?" Otto stamped his foot on the ground.

Ellinor was already near the corner of the street, about thirty yards further on.

The strange person wearing the dark welding goggles stood peeling an apple under the lilac tree.

"You should take the cigars with you. He's very fond of them."

Otto started back up the street involuntarily.

"Who are you?" he whispered.

"I'm one of those people with a driver's license," said the man who looked like a woman. Or the other way around.

Otto looked tensely in Ellinor's direction just as she disappeared round the corner.

"If you hurry, we'll just make it."

Did the voice come from the mouth of the woman? Or did it just hang there in the air? Otto took a step forward.

"Are you talking about Grandfather?" he asked softly.

The peelings from the small round apple lay like a spiral on the floor.

"Are you going to get them, Noa?" said the voice.

Otto started to run. First backward, then sideways, and finally forward and at full speed back to his entrance, up the stairs, into the apartment where there was the smell of the evening meal, the noise of the television, his mother's sewing machine, and thirteen years of dust, all of it Otto's.

His parents were sitting in the living room. He went to his own room and closed the door behind him. In less than a minute, his mother was standing in the doorway asking what had happened to Ellinor. Otto was afraid the conversation would end up the same way as it had a few times before—why he never brought friends home with him, why he never went to anyone's house, why he did not choose a sport. It always ended with his mother saying, "It's a year ago now, Otto."

"I think Ellinor's rather ill-mannered. But perhaps that goes with being a punk," said his mother. She pushed the door open so Otto could see the hall.

"We've got a trash can here." His mother kept her arms folded. "So madam doesn't have to throw her garbage onto the mat."

Otto looked at the beige-colored coconut matting where the apple peelings lay in the shape of a spiral. Mother picked up the peelings and took them to the kitchen. Meanwhile, Otto went to the drawer in his father's desk, took the cigar box, and hid it in his windbreaker. "What on earth's happening?" he whispered to himself as he opened the front door. Ten minutes later he was at the hedge under the white lilac—where of course there was no one to be seen.

"Hello. Is there anyone there?" he cried. "It's me. Otto."

He turned round as quick as lightning when the car stopped

behind him with a sigh. It was gray and of a make unknown to Otto. The driver, on the other hand, he knew very well.

The back seat is soft, almost too soft. There is a strange smell hanging inside the car, sweet but at the same time sharp, a smell that makes you feel sick, a rancid smell. They are on their way. The car drives at a considerable speed. It is only now that Otto notices that there is a window between himself and the driver. They pass a big green meadow with a beautiful lavender-blue sky above it. Hundreds of strange animals are grazing on the grass. Reddish-brown colored animals with white stomachs standing on thin, uncertain legs. Enormous chestnut animals.

Suddenly the car stops. The door is opened. Or it opens on its own.

A cold, clammy air surrounds him. An air that smells strongly of rust and oil, of rubber and seawater. The water between the road and the shipyard is pitch black.

A small boat sails toward them. As if something suddenly occurs to him, he holds his hand out to the driver. "You mustn't touch me, Noa," says the driver. A minute later Otto is sitting in the motorboat behind an elderly man wearing blue overalls. They cruise into a big dock and pass an enormous rusty-brown ship on which the name is just being painted. F E O . . . , it says. The painter is standing on a sort of swing. He is whistling a melody that echoes through the funnel-shaped entrance.

"Be careful of the crane, Noa," says the man in the boat, pointing upward.

"Be careful of the crane, Noa," it echoes through the dock as if a hundred men are talking in deep voices.

The big crane turns inward above the bow of the ship; a heavy chest is hanging on the shiny cable. The crane looks just like a sort of lizard with a big case in its mouth. The boat moors. Otto looks at the black water, which shines unnaturally.

"Why does the water look so strange?" he asks the man, who is sitting with his back toward him.

"Oil," he answers. "Oil has leaked. An accident."

"Oil. Oil has leaked. An accident," it echoes from all sides, like a choir.

"What should I do?" cries Otto.

"Just follow the crane," answers the man, who cruises away in his little boat.

Otto clasps his hands round the cigar box and starts walking. Staring above at the black silhouette of the enormous crane.

Suddenly he stops. A flame lights up in the dark. Enormous shadows of men running along the bow of the ship set everything in motion. A siren begins to blare. Otto stares at the workers wearing blue overalls who are walking all over the place. Only now does he discover that the water is on fire. He starts to run too. Round and round. A labyrinth. The water is on fire. In a number of places, thick blue columns of smoke swirl upward shaped like cyclones. The sound of motors screeching as they are being started up. Otto is walking on a sort of tarpaulin. The material yields and he gets no further. He looks up to where the top of the crane is half hidden by the smoke. But the chest, the chest on the thick cable, is still dangling above the dock. Otto looks at the palms of his hands, which are red with blood. It is coming out of tiny cuts. Suddenly, somebody appears by the bow of the ship. The way the man moves—Otto blinks and slowly shakes his head from side to side.

"Grandfather," he whispers.

"What on earth are you doing?"

He looked up at Ellinor's white face. At Ellinor's green hair.

He was lying on the ground under the lilac tree.

"Have you started smoking?"

"Smoking?"

She took the box of cigars from his hands. "Unbelievably stupid, Otto. Cigars!"

He shook his head and looked at the palms of his hands.

Ellinor said that cigars like that could make you feel dizzy.

Otto asked her if she had seen a gray car too.

"Come on, your head between your knees. You're as pale as death, man."

Ellinor had something of the commander about her, and Otto chose to obey. She said that she had suddenly noticed that he was gone.

"Then I came back and saw you lying here snoozing. It could be anemia too. You're trembling all over, Otto."

Otto mumbled that it would be better if he went home. Ellinor went all the way back with him, this time on the same side of the road. They stood together in front of the entrance to the stairs.

"You'd better stop smoking those cigars. I can smell them all over you."

"I haven't been smoking," said Otto quietly.

Ellinor took a step back. "You can smell it a mile away. Bye."

Sunday. They drove to the new house on the coast, where painters and carpenters had been working for two weeks. Otto followed his mother from room to room. She said she was thrilled with the light which fell on the bare floor in geometrical shapes. His father was talking to a landscape gardener who was knowledgeable about bamboo hedges.

On the second floor his mother opened the door to a large room that looked out onto the sea. There was a big old wardrobe and a wicker chair from more recent times. An oval mirror hung on the wall; it had an old golden frame.

"Nice, isn't it, Otto? Twice as big as your old room. And especially nice for you who so love sitting on the windowsill! You'll see, you'll make a few friends here in the neighborhood. It's high time you started joining in again."

His father called from the garden. His mother went downstairs. Otto counted the stairs. Eighteen altogether. It was indeed a nice room. But he would rather have a view of other houses, of chimneys and shops, of people in cozy flats; in a strange way, the view of the woods and the coast was too neat for him. Like a chessboard without chessmen. Without a clock. He put his knapsack on the bare floor. His school bag containing the pocket chess game with magnetic chessmen, his Walkman, and the cigar box. He had a plan. A plan that entailed hiding the box of cigars here in the house. So that it would not disappear in the big cleanup before the move.

He turned round and looked at himself in the mirror with damp spots on it. I have red cheeks, he said to himself. Ellinor had asked for his new address, but Otto had not yet given it to her. He had nothing against her company, but he just preferred being alone. He walked over to the mirror and suddenly shrank back. Began breathing more quickly. The strange man stood behind him. Or woman. Behind him or in the mirror.

It was as if Otto's feet were stuck to the ground. He could not turn round.

"You decide, Noa."

"Go away."

"Do you mean that?"

"What do you want from me?"

"Your grandfather has something for you."

"My grandfather's dead. Why won't you understand that? He's dead. For more than a year now."

"A year, two months, and five days."

The stranger put his hands in his pockets. Otto gave him a wide berth and went to the door. Eighteen stairs down. Into the garden, where his mother stood next to his father. They smiled. Asked if he wanted to walk with them to the water. Otto said nothing and looked indirectly at the big wooden house with the high narrow windows. Found his own window, where there was a shadow lying across the windowsill.

"I hate that old mirror," he said.

"But then we'll hang it somewhere else."

"I think you should throw it away."

"Otto, what's the matter with you?"

"Now, right away! I think it's nasty. If I've definitely got to have that room in that dreadful house, at least take that mirror away. Now."

"Yes, but, dear . . . !" Mommy laughed, baffled.

Otto's father put his arm round him and dragged him into the house. "If you don't want it there, we'll take it away."

They went up the eighteen stairs. His father opened the door to Otto's room. Otto remained in the hall. Heard his father taking the mirror from the wall. He came out of the room with it. "Is his lordship satisfied now?"

Otto looked past his father into the room. The sun was so low now that it shone directly onto the wall, where you could clearly see the shadow of a man.

"There's someone inside there," whispered Otto.

"Inside where, Otto?"

"Inside the room."

His father smiled at him and pushed the door wide open. At

that moment the light disappeared.

"I can't see anyone. Do you think it's haunted here?"

"No, it's not haunted," mumbled Otto, who had never believed in ghosts.

The oval-shaped mirror stood in the hall now, against the paneling. Otto could see the stranger in the mirror. Then she must be standing in his parents' bedroom. His father said something. At least, his mouth moved.

"We're going for a walk to the beach. Are you coming with us, Otto? Can you hear me?"

Otto looked down and shook his head. "I'm staying here. By the way, it doesn't matter about the mirror."

His father laughed and threw his arms round him. Said that he had a son who presented mankind with riddles. Otto threw his arms round his father's neck. And he saw how the stranger nodded and smiled. As if it suited her well.

"Father, actually . . ."

"Yes, Otto."

"Can't you tell me, without it getting complicated, exactly how Grandfather died?"

"Oh, Otto. Why do you keep starting on about that? I'm so tired of it. You should put that business about grandfather behind you. Are you coming with me to the beach? Then you'll get some fresh air."

Otto repeated his question.

Otto's father responded to the question. He turned round, stretched his arms, sighed, and said, "It was an accident. At the shipyard. I believe it began with an oil leak. Everyone tried to get away, but there were flames everywhere. And toxic fumes."

"The water's on fire," whispered Otto.

"I don't really know exactly how it happened. Perhaps

Grandfather tried to get away too. But when the fire had been extinguished and they went looking for possible survivors, they found him. We were told that something had probably fallen on his head. You see, he never wore a helmet."

"He's still there," Otto whispered to himself. "Poor Grandfather's still there. He can't get away."

Otto went and sat on the windowsill and saw his parents disappear between the trees. A gray car stopped in front of the house. Otto took his knapsack and went down the eighteen stairs to the front door.

He stares through the windshield. Either it is misty or they are driving through a tunnel in the form of a three-dimensional spider's web. Perhaps, he thought, we are not moving forward at all. There is no noise coming from the motor, he can feel no bumps or vibrations, and strangely enough, they are going straight on all the time. They are just sitting there while something outside is moving past them.

Suddenly the door opens. Otto steps out and sees the same spectacle as the last time. Everything is yellow and black. The little motorboat rocks on the burning water. They are in a hurry now. Otto looks up at the painter, still busy painting the name of the ship. Now it says F E O D . . . People walk past each other without having any real contact. Otto can see the crane turning; it comes to hang above the dock. The chest on the cable. Otto starts to run. A whole group of men approaches him. Heavy clouds of smoke swirl upward like cyclones. Otto stands still and sees his grandfather wearing his worn overalls. He is standing there as if he has been waiting for this moment for months. One year, two months, and five days. As if his feet have been sewn to the floor. But Otto has to keep an eye on the crane all the time, the crane with the big heavy chest and the cable with flames crawling up it like snails.

"Grandfather."

"Put them down there on the floor, Noa."

"But Grandfather, I . . . "

Otto looks at the palms of his hands, which are starting to bleed again.

"Quick, my boy. I can't stay standing here much longer. I've got something for you. A promise is a promise."

Otto is groping around in his knapsack when the sound of a steel wire breaking cuts through the dock. The cable has burned through. Straight across the middle. For one second, the sirens are silent. In that second, Otto stares at the heavy chest floating freely through the air. Like one of a pair of colossal dice rolling round and round. As if in slow motion.

"The chest!" Otto shouts to his grandfather. Their eyes meet. In the one second. Life and death clash with one another. Time and place.

"What are you doing, Otto?"

He looked up at his mother, who was standing next to him with a bouquet of yellow St. John's wort. On his hands and knees, Otto gathered up his small magnetic chessmen, which were strewn all over the floor.

"I dropped them."

"Did you drop them? You were rooting about in the soil. Is something the matter, Otto? What on earth is that smell?"

"Nothing." He took three strides backward, but his mother followed him. Daddy was already sitting in the car hooting impatiently.

"Have you been smoking?"

"Of course I haven't been smoking."

"Your clothes smell of smoke."

"Then that's because of the house."

She looked at him. Suspiciously, as if she wanted to say, I'm not giving up, I will certainly find out what you have been up to.

He saw Ellinor again in the reading room at the library. By coincidence, they were sitting opposite each other, both of them with big atlases in front of them. Otto's eyes wandered round the beautiful reading room, along the hanging lamps, the green upholstered tables, the books that stood on the shelves shoulder to shoulder.

"Ellinor," whispered Otto. "You can keep a secret, can't you?"

Ellinor answered that she was not exactly a gossip.

Otto put his atlas down and looked at her. "Sometimes I'm picked up by a strange gray car, by a strange person, something somewhere in between a man and a woman. I don't know whether the car moves forward or not or if the things around the car move, but suddenly I'm in my grandfather's old shipyard. On the spot where he was killed. I have his cigars with me. That's what it's all about. I think. You're the only one I dare tell. Am I going mad? I'm almost afraid to be alone now."

Ellinor looked around her. "Put your head under the cold tap. And your wrists. You're certainly not the only one."

"No?"

"Last October, I was involved in geckos, you know, lizards. I used to walk around at night. Very annoying. We have that sort of thing inside us. We think we are made of flesh and blood alone, with a cauliflower head and a memory. I'm telling you, Otto, there's more to it than that. Lots more. Much scarier things. Much deeper too."

"To be honest," Otto said, shaking his head slowly from one side to the other, "I think this is something different. Do you know, those cigars, they mean something. They're a passport or something like it."

"Perhaps you want to smoke on the sly."

"Absolutely not. But they remind me of him. My grandfather. The smell. I'm almost addicted to it."

"Then you'd better make sure you get rid of that addiction. It's all getting much too heavy."

Otto nodded. "I think I've thought of a way," he said. "I've made a decision. I've thrown them into one of those big trash bags at home. Where we put everything that we don't want to take with us. Now I haven't got anything they want. And that's an end to that strange person in that peculiar gray car. It wasn't easy, but it's done now. The bags are being collected today."

"Exactly," said Ellinor. "In the end game, you have to let them see who's really the boss."

"I just have the feeling that I've disappointed him." Otto lay his head on the table.

"Your grandfather?"

"Yes, my grandfather. He wanted the cigars so badly."

"Perhaps," said Ellinor, tired, "perhaps he needs the cigars to move on further."

Otto looked at her.

Ellinor said, "Perhaps he's stuck."

"Stuck—how do you mean?"

"Well, I don't know what's going on with you. I've got my own problems. But perhaps he can't move on further. Perhaps he misses his cigars. A car can't run without gas, can it, and a clock has to be wound up."

Otto stared at her and then stood up. "Ellinor," he said quickly, "you're fantastic, just fantastic."

"Well, don't rattle on about it."

He ran. At the most, it was only a few miles from the library to his home. But it could all be a question of minutes, perhaps seconds even. Round the corner. His feet on the asphalt. I'm coming, he whispered to himself, I'm coming. I'll definitely be on time. The truck stood in front of their door. The blue smoke came out of the exhaust in small puffs, like little coughs.

"Wait," he cried. "Wait!" He caught sight of his mother standing on the pavement.

Otto felt the pain in his lungs and his thighs.

"Wait," he screamed as he ran to the side of the truck.

The man behind the steering wheel stared at him. Now his mother joined them. Asked what on earth was the matter.

"A misunderstanding," panted Otto. "Sorry, but I must . . ."

The man said he had other things to do. Otto climbed into the back. There were at least fifty gray bags. It was the huge garbage truck. With masses of old trash. His mother asked him to come down, and the driver, who was very cross, came out of his cab.

"What are you looking for Otto?" said his mother.

Otto already had his head halfway into a big gray bag. The wrong one.

"Come down, man." The driver was preparing to climb into the back personally in order to throw Otto out. Then Otto caught sight of the box. He could see its shape quite clearly through the plastic bag. He tipped the bag upside down. Now the man was definitely coming. He was furious. Otto couldn't care less.

"Come down, Otto," his mother called now too. The man grabbed Otto by his collar just as Otto caught sight of the gray car rolling toward them silently from the other side of the street. Otto grabbed the cigar box out of the trash and jumped onto the pavement. Landed right at his mother's feet. She stared at him in incomprehension.

"This is unhealthy," she said.

Otto nodded. "Maybe it is," he said. "But it's nearly over."

The truck drove away. Otto saw his mother disappear through the doorway, and he walked to the gray car.

On the way he keeps his eyes closed. Holds the cigar box and tries to prepare himself for what is to come. Says to himself that it will probably all work out. The panic at the shipyard is now complete. Ambulances, fire engines, and rescue workers walking round among the injured shipyard workers. Everyone stares at the flames. Otto walks along the bow of the ship to the half-burned swing where, just a minute ago, a painter had stood painting the name on the ship. The crane appears above Otto's head. The cable is burning.

"Noa."

Otto stands still, looks at his grandfather, who is still standing in the same place as before. "Grandfather," he whispers. "Be careful of the chest, be careful, Grandfather."

Otto says it even though he knows it will make no difference. That there is no escaping it.

"Put the box down there, my boy."

Otto puts the box down in front of him.

Now the cable breaks. With an enormous bang. But something rolls along across the soft, bumpy asphalt, something that shines like copper and sounds like metal. Otto picks up the key and everything disappears in a sulphur-colored cloud of smoke.

The flat was now almost empty. Father tidied up the bathroom while mother packed their clothes. Now they were only waiting for the three moving men who would come and collect their last things. The stereo, the television, and the longcase clock with the hands that never moved.

Otto walks round saying farewell to everything. Not least of all to the light and the shadows on the wall. Finally he opens the square-shaped window and puts the copper key into the old clock. Turns it round eight times.

All the way round. All the way round.

The old clock groans and cracks. Then the sound comes, *tick-tock, tick-tock, tick-tock, tick-tock*. He moves the hands so that they are in the same position as the hands on his watch.

Otto puts the key into his pocket.

Shortly afterward, the three moving men are standing in the doorway. They are perspiring but look friendly. They lift up the clock and carry it very carefully down the stairs.

"Careful," says Otto. "You can cut yourselves on the sides."

On the way down, the clock strikes twelve and plays a short frail melody.

In the bathroom, his father lifts his head up, and in the bedroom, his mother puts her hand to her mouth in shock.

But Otto goes and sits on the windowsill.

It is a beautiful summer's day. A rope comes down from the sky. That is how it should be. It will always hang there like the rope on a church bell. No more and no less. Otto jumps off the windowsill and pulls the small envelope out of his back pocket. Goes to the mailbox and sees the letter disappear.

> Dear Ellinor,
> We moved today. I am pleased with our

new house. Think you should come for a visit sometime. As you can see, I have enclosed a small chestnut. It feels good in your hands.

All best wishes,

Otto.

P.S. I'm also pleased with my new green hair.

Uri Orlev

The Song of the Whales

When Michael was little, his grandfather Mr. Hammermann came three times a week to play with him or to go out for a walk. And if his grandfather was late, Michael waited for him outside on the street, even when winter had set in. But when his grandfather could no longer leave his house, Michael learned how to go alone by bus—he was in the first class at school at that time—and then he was the one who went visiting at his grandfather's home. There were lots of reasons for going visiting there, lots to see and lots to do, enough for more than one visit, enough for a visit lasting a week and more. Mr. Hammermann was an antique dealer, and in his house there were two stories that were furnished as if they were lived in, just for the show. In reality, the many rooms were occupied solely by valuable furniture and other things that came and went. Michael was deeply impressed by the abundance of splendid objects and collections, all of which had their own stories too.

In one cupboard, his grandfather kept broken toys that Michael was not allowed to touch and some battered games that he was not allowed to play with because they dated all the way back to his grandfather's youth. And his grandfather's youth was so long ago that for a child, it seemed like a thousand years. When he came, Michael liked roaming around the house with his grandfather. He liked opening forgotten drawers and cupboards that had not been opened for years, and he liked asking questions. His grandfather had endless patience and always answered all his questions. To their amazement, they sometimes discovered rooms that had been completely forgotten, but the grandfather and Michael were not afraid of dust and cobwebs. Madame Sibonnier was always happy when they had found a room like that, for she was always looking for things that needed cleaning. She always cleaned everything that needed cleaning, even the grandfather.

Madame Sibonnier was the housekeeper. In private, Michael called her "Soap-oh-dear." His grandfather nearly died laughing when Michael told him about the nickname. At first she did not give the small guest a warm welcome. On his first visits she had even tricked him secretly. When he rang the bell, she watched him from behind the curtains but did not open the door. Since his grandfather did not hear the bell, Michael stood there waiting in front of the door in vain. Finally the truth came out and the grandfather was very angry with her.

"I didn't hear the bell," said Madame Sibonnier very sweetly.

Another time, she let Michael into the drawing room downstairs but did not tell Mr. Hammermann that his grandson was waiting for him. And it was only when he began to call "Grandpa, Grandpa!" that his grandfather realized Michael was there. The housekeeper got a scolding.

"I'd forgotten. I'm sorry," she said in an aggrieved voice.

"Jeanette wants me all to herself," Mr. Hammermann had once said angrily. He was talking to himself, but Michael heard him.

"Grandpa, why don't you dismiss her?"

"I promised Grandma," said the grandfather. "And anyway . . ." he added a short while later with a knowing smile.

Michael did not understand the meaning of that but he did not ask.

"Don't worry," said the grandfather. "Jeanette'll get used to you."

And it is true, it was not long before Madame Sibonnier began to clean up Michael too. He was hardly inside when Madame Sibonnier pulled off his shoes to polish them. While he waited, she gave him old slippers belonging to his grandfather. She brushed his clothes, and in the winter she dried and brushed his coat too. She also made an attempt to clean his ears with a cotton ball and his nose too, but Michael stood his ground and refused. Even so, she managed to clean one ear the first time she caught him unexpectedly.

One of the rooms in Grandfather's big house was called the library. From the floor to the ceiling, there was nothing but books. The grandfather always put his grandson in an armchair so big and so soft that he almost disappeared in it and then read him stories or told him about the photographs in the family albums. In this way, Michael also got to know his grandmother, who had died before he was born. Madame Sibonnier also liked to come into the library because the books, she always said, collected dust, and she loved removing that dust. In another room, where the walls had been paneled with wood, there was a gramophone and cupboards full of gramophone records. It was called the music room. When the grandfather let Michael listen to records, Madame Sibonnier often came and sat with them there to listen too. Unlike the books, which could not be washed, Madame Sibonnier washed all the gramophone records now and again after taking them out of their sleeves. Then she let them dry on blotting paper. There was one gramophone record that Michael loved especially—it was the one with the singing of the whales.

When Michael was nine years old, Mr. Hammermann's health began to deteriorate, and Michael's parents managed to persuade him to sell his house and move in with them. There were three unoccupied nurseries in their house because they had only had one child, and that was Michael. The solicitor, Mr. Hammermann's trusted representative, sold Mr. Hammermann's house and most of the things in it at a big auction sale. Much was written about it in the newspapers, and there was even something about it in the news on television. At the same time as the grandfather moved in, a few paintings in gilt frames, a few objets d'art, and a few things that did not interest Michael were brought over to his parents' house.

Mr. Hammermann got the first in the line of nurseries, Madame Sibonnier got the room next to that, and Michael remained in his own room. After the grandfather had been living with them for a while, it became clear that he had an extraordinary gift that Michael had not discovered before. It changed his whole life in one swoop. The discovery came about when once, suddenly afraid of the monsters of the night, Michael ran to his grandfather's room and crawled under the blankets with him—he was not allowed to sleep with his father and mother—and noticed that his grandfather was able to take Michael with him into his dreams. From that night on, Michael very often went and slept with his grandfather, not bothered by the snoring, the coughing, and the smells or by Madame Sibonnier's desperate attempts to keep him out. If she could have, she would have slept in front of old Mr. Hammermann's door as the slaves did in front of their masters' doors generations before, but the house was not designed for sleeping habits like that. It is true, she always left the door to her room half-open so that she could prevent Michael from crawling into bed with his grandfather, but when Michael came creeping past her room, he always heard her snoring.

"All children are dirty," she said.

Since she, together with the old man, had come to live with

the family, she did not have enough rooms and things to clean anymore, and she had thrown herself into cleaning the same rooms and the same things time and time again, day in and day out. The occupants of the house and of course Michael in particular were the greatest enemies of cleanliness. Madame Sibonnier was given permission by Michael's mother to bathe him and wash him every day when he returned from school covered with dirt, not to mention all the viruses and bacteria he was breathing in when he was with other children. But Michael was not a child anymore. He simply refused and said that he was embarrassed by the strange woman. Finally it was agreed that he would wash himself every evening. Michael hated washing himself, so usually he just pretended to be doing it. He locked himself in the bathroom, turned on the tap to satisfy Soap-oh-dear, who was all ears, and before he came out he rubbed some soap behind his ears and some toothpaste in his mouth. That was not such a nice taste, but he rinsed out his mouth immediately afterward and that way he smelt clean to Soap-oh-dear. Then he lay in bed waiting. He tried to keep his eyes open. As soon as he heard Madame Sibonnier coming out of the shower and opening the door from the hall to her room, he knew that she would be fast asleep within five minutes.

Michael did not always manage to stay awake, but if he did succeed, it was worth it. His grandfather did not let him down once and always took Michael with him into his dreams. Sometimes they were short and then Michael went on with his own ordinary dreams, but sometimes the dreams were long and compelling. Certain parts of them were not in fact real dreams. They were, as his grandfather explained to him, slight distortions of reality. Michael did not understand that scholarly explanation, but before long he preferred those slight distortions to everything else, even to watching television or playing computer games and definitely to studying the cello. His father was a cellist in an orchestra and hoped that Michael would become at least as famous a cellist as Pablo Casals, but Michael preferred his grandfather's dreams to any other occupation and he preferred his grandfather's company to any other company.

As soon as they were both awake, Michael had usually forgotten the dreams that his grandfather had allowed him to share, but sometimes when he opened his eyes he could still feel the excitement and the tension and sometimes the dreadful fear that a moment before had paralyzed his legs and almost strangled him. Even though the dreams had been forgotten, a few vague images usually remained in his memory and disappeared as the day went on. But one of the images Michael did not forget, even though he and his grandfather had only been there once. They approached a house that stood between tall trees. His grandfather took him by the hand. They arrived there just before evening, and the trees were already in darkness. They walked past a staircase with a few steps that led to a lighted entrance and a front door which was open. There were people sitting on the steps. You could see inside one of the rooms through the open door. A number of figures could be seen, some sitting on chairs, others hanging on a couch or leaning in an armchair. Some of them were sitting by a fire, others were leaning with their elbows on the windowsill. Everyone who was there remained engraved in Michael's memory. He remembered them all, men, women, and children, and he remembered exactly what everyone was doing at that moment, what they were wearing, their hairstyle, the expression on their face. Michael knew the people and the house very well, although he had never been there before and had never met anyone there.

With one of his dreams Mr. Hammermann made his grandson quite distressed. He had invented a machine that could make time stand still. He used his invention, and time just stood still. At first everyone was happy. They celebrated and crowned the grandfather as king and emperor. But gradually the elation declined because a few years went by and nothing changed. Everything remained as it had been when the grandfather put his invention into operation. The same young birds remained in the nest, the same mother and father birds went on feeding their young. The same grandmothers went on shaking their tablecloths out of the windows. The same children went on going to nursery school or to school, everyone to their own class. Until everyone had had enough. And one day Michael's grandfather came into his grandson's room and saw him crying bitterly.

"Why are you crying, Michael?" asked the grandfather, who as king and emperor could give his grandson anything he wanted.

"Grandpa," said Michael, "I'll never grow up, I'll never be a father."

Michael woke up in his grandfather's bed crying bitterly. The grandfather woke up too and lay there sadly.

"But it wasn't a scary dream," he said apologetically.

Michael could not put into words why he was crying. The problem was that he did not know what he wanted, to grow big and strong, to ride in a sports car and not be frightened of monsters at night—for he still thought then that adults are not afraid at night—or to stay nine years old forever so that his grandfather would never die.

After his grandfather had a dream about flying, Michael understood for the first time what his grandfather meant when he said that sometimes his dreams were not ordinary but were distortions of reality. They both stepped onto a bicycle and started to pedal fast. At first they rode straight along the road, but then suddenly it happened—they began to take off. With great effort, they managed to ride through the air. But the wonder did not last, just as when young birds try to fly for the first time. They landed on the ground again, and Michael felt a choking disappointment in his throat. His grandfather did not give up. They made a new attempt, and this time the uncertainty about their own abilities changed to a feeling of certainty and of command over a power about which there was no doubt. They did not have to strain anymore. They had the flying completely under control, and Michael was filled with the joy of clear air stretching as far as the horizon. They flew over the whole length of the valley, which was so beautiful that no words could describe it.

"This is just like in the film *ET!*" said Michael, full of zest.

"But not quite the same," said his grandfather.

At that moment Michael realized that he could not ride a bicycle at all, and immediately he fell with a thud to the ground.

"Luckily, not on the road," his grandfather said, still in the dream. When they were both awake, his grandfather said, "Michael, if you want to fly with me again in this dream, you'll have to learn to ride a bicycle."

"All right, Grandpa," said Michael.

It seldom happened that Michael agreed to anything. Usually he answered with a "no," but if it was about his grandfather's dreams, everything was different. It took three weeks before Michael's broken leg could be taken out of the cast. Then, by telephone, Mr. Hammermann ordered a bicycle that Michael liked from the catalog of a mail-order firm, completely against the will of Michael's parents. They thought he was still too small and were afraid that he would be run over. Of course, grandfather and grandson did not tell them why it was necessary for Michael to be able to ride a bicycle.

He had trouble learning to ride the bicycle for some time after it arrived. It was only when his uncle Nimrod suggested a different method that Michael tried again and managed to do it. The method consisted of two steps. First you had to hold the bicycle with one hand on the saddle and the other hand on the handlebars and walk with it. That was nice because a lot of neighbors and their children who met Michael in the street were convinced he had just got off his new bicycle for a minute and was walking a short distance for his own enjoyment and that it went without saying he could ride a bicycle very well. The second step was that you sat on the saddle and, without touching the pedals, rode down a gentle slope. The saddle had to be low enough so you could reach the ground with your feet at any moment. And it was true, Michael learned how to ride a bicycle after practicing for six weeks, and from that moment on there were no more problems when his grandfather had another flying dream.

Everything became more difficult when both of Michael's parents went abroad. His mother had to go to a convention for psychiatrists and his father went on tour with his orchestra, and they left Michael and his grandfather in the care of Madame Sibonnier. The very first evening, she walked into the bathroom as soon as Michael had finished "washing" himself and noticed that all the towels were still dry. She felt the soap and the toothbrush, and everything was as dry as a bone. Madame Sibonnier went to the storage room, took out a camp bed, put it in front of the door to the old man's room, and made it up to sleep in. Michael was not allowed to go in.

The following evening, before Grandfather went to sleep, he went to Michael to give him a good-night kiss and then took him with him to his own room. He took Michael in bed with him, despite the objections from Madame Sibonnier. Now, for the first time, she began to suspect that the boy was not sleeping with the old man just because of night monsters. In the first years after Mrs. Hammermann's death, Madame Sibonnier was the one Mr. Hammermann took with him into his dreams. Then one day he told her that it was over. He explained to her that he had lost his gift. Madame Sibonnier was very distressed that their special bond was broken, but she believed him.

Now she was lying on the camp bed with her ear against the closed door, and even though the conversation inside was being carried out in whispers, she was shocked. Many years had passed since her exclusion from Mr. Hammermann's dreams, but her soul was still deeply wounded. She jumped off the camp bed and pushed it away from the door furiously. Through the strength of the push, the bed fell over and noisily folded double on the floor. Madame Sibonnier stormed into the room wearing just her night-dress, with her hair disheveled, and she dragged Michael out without taking any notice of his protests. Only now did Michael notice how big and strong she was.

"We'll put this right, don't worry," the grandfather said to Michael the next day.

"When, Grandpa?"

"Even before your parents come back."

Michael waited patiently.

Mr. Hammermann stopped washing himself, did not brush his teeth anymore, and did not put on clean clothes or socks anymore. He went to sleep without putting on his pajamas and went to bed wearing the clothes he had worn during the day. He did not even take off his slippers. When his grandfather did not wash himself anymore, Michael did not either, despite the protests from Madame Sibonnier. Michael refused to put on clean clothes too. He was especially stubborn about socks. He was prepared to comb his hair, but he resisted cleaning his teeth with all his might. The problem of the clothes was much worse for him than for his grandfather. Madame Sibonnier snapped them up as soon as she had the chance, soaked them in the sink or the bathtub, and threw them in the washing machine. So Michael did not put his pajamas on at night anymore and went to bed with his clothes on. A few of his classmates began calling him "stink-pot." Michael couldn't care less. He did not know what would happen next because his grandfather had not yet told him what would happen in the dream for which they were preparing themselves so thoroughly.

After three days Madame Sibonnier was walking around with wads of cotton in her nose. She was very nervous and seemed to know that something terrible was about to happen. But she was not prepared to make the slightest compromise.

"He's not sleeping in your bed!" she stated at every opportunity.

Mr. Hammermann came to Michael's room each evening to give him a good-night kiss and to see if he smelled enough. It was only after another week that he bent over Michael and said, "Excellent."

He went to his room and after quite a while came back very softly carrying his pillows. Michael awoke when his grandfather got into bed with him and pulled at the blankets.

"Where is she?" Michael asked sleepily.

"Fallen asleep," answered the grandfather.

He had lain down on the outside so that Michael would not fall out of the narrow bed. It was not long before they were walking together through the streets of the empty city. Suddenly Michael noticed that there were small creatures following them that had come out of dustbins and containers and even out of the drains along the curb.

"Grandpa, something's following us."

"I know. Do you know the story of the Pied Piper of Hamelin?"

Michael knew that story.

"But Grandpa, you haven't got a pipe."

"That's right," answered the grandfather, "but I've got music from smells."

And it was true. In the light from the street lamp, Michael could see a strange sort of light that followed them like a tail. He stood still for a moment and walked into the transparent wake that his grandfather left behind him. The stench filled his nose. Then he bent over to see what kind of black creatures they were that whirled when the wind blew behind them with their quivering, threadlike legs and feelers.

"Grandpa, those aren't mice," said Michael.

"I know," said the grandfather. "This is our army to drive Madame Sibonnier away with."

The troops continued to build up. The little black creatures ran quickly after them and climbed onto them and into their trouser legs. Full of disgust, Michael shook them off himself again, and again and finally he began to run. His grandfather ran too, like a man of twenty, and the black creatures kept frantically close on their heels. There were even a few among them that flew a distance so as not to lag behind the rest. Following Michael and his grandfather, the creatures climbed up the steps to the house. When Mr. Hammermann opened the door, they all pushed their way inside. Michael and his grandfather stood still, pressing themselves against the wall in the hall and waiting. At first, nothing happened. They stood still even though thousands of tiny legs were running across the floor. Then there was a shriek, and

Madame Sibonnier came running out of her room, absolutely desperate, with an aerosol can full of poison in each hand. She sprayed the cockroaches furiously and stamped on them, even though she loathed the disgusting sound of the cracking bodies, but there were too many of them. When she slipped on the flattened cockroaches and fell on the floor, they climbed onto her and covered her until she looked like a big crawling black hill, and she was unable to get up.

"Grandpa," shouted Michael, "wake up, wake up!"

Someone was shouting close to his ear. Michael listened for a moment and then understood that it was he who was shouting. He quieted down and felt next to him in the bed, but his grandfather was not there. From behind the heavy curtains, the morning light was shining in. Michael got up and ran to his grandfather's room. He did not meet Madame Sibonnier on the way. On the floor, there were flattened lumps of cockroach here and there. Michael looked at them with disgust. He walked carefully between them and went to his grandfather's room. Mr. Hammermann was not there. On the way back, Michael passed the bathroom and heard someone having a shower.

"Grandpa?"

Mr. Hammermann did not hear him because of the strong jet of water from the shower under which he was standing. Quickly Michael went to the kitchen to see if Madame Sibonnier had prepared breakfast for them. She was not there. Dead cockroaches were lying everywhere in the kitchen too. Michael ran to Madame Sibonnier's room. The door was closed. He turned the handle. The door opened. He went inside—the room was empty. He walked over to the wardrobe to open it. He hesitated for a minute—all her clothes had disappeared. Then he turned round and saw his grandfather standing in the doorway, wearing a bathrobe.

"Grandpa?"

Mr. Hammermann smiled at him and said, "Go and have a shower, Michael. It's time you did!"

Dead cockroaches lay on the bathroom floor too. Michael flushed them down the drain. He dressed carefully. This was the first time in his life that he enjoyed putting on clean clothes. When he walked up the staircase, he found some cockroaches there hiding in dark corners. Michael pretended they were not there. He could still hear the sound of the cracking of their bodies when Madame Sibonnier stamped on them, and he did not feel like a repeat performance.

He was not too late for school, but lesson by lesson it became more difficult for him to listen and give answers to the questions. All the time, the great armies of cockroaches that his grandfather had brought home were going through his head, and his brain was tortured by the question: Had they eaten her up? Had they really eaten her up? Do cockroaches eat people? No, that could not be true. In the biology lesson he held up his hand and asked, "Sir, do cockroaches eat people?"

The whole class burst out laughing.

"At the moment, Michael, we're not dealing with the order of Dictyoptera in the insect class. But I think that humans would be a rather large prey for them. Except if you made very small crumbs of them."

After that answer, it cost the teacher a great deal of effort to calm down the class, which was roaring with laughter.

As soon as the last bell rang, Michael ran home. There was no trace of the cockroaches. The house was as clean as if Madame Sibonnier were still in charge.

"I had the pest control and a cleaning crew in," Grandfather explained.

When Michael's parents came home, they found it difficult to believe that the old man had had an argument with Madame Sibonnier and that she had left. But because she did not contact them and nobody talked about her, they employed a young woman who took over all Madame Sibonnier's duties.

One evening when Michael came to sleep with his grandfather, the old man gave him a strange key and said that he should take great care of it. Michael's curiosity was roused, but he asked no questions. The grandfather turned the night-light off next to the bed, and they lay silently with their eyes closed.

"Where's the key?"

"I've got it in my hand," said Michael.

"Good," said his grandfather. "Hold it tight."

The grandfather was in a good mood. They went and drank tea in the library in his old house. When Michael heard footsteps approaching with a noise like slippers shuffling along, he was convinced that Madame Sibonnier would soon appear, but an old woman Michael did not know came in. It took some time before he recognized her from the photographs of his grandmother in the family album. And sure enough, his grandfather called her by her name. There was nothing scary about her, but even so, Michael was worried, for she had died before he was born. He kept feeling to make sure he still had the key in his hand, although he had no idea what he was supposed to use it for.

The grandmother took absolutely no notice of him. She looked angry and said to his grandfather, "Johann, why did you dismiss Jeanette?"

Michael was surprised. Nobody called his grandfather by his first name. They called him Father or Grandfather or Mr. Hammermann.

"I didn't dismiss her," said the grandfather laughingly. "But it's true, we had an argument and I'm rid of her."

"You promised me that you'd let her stay as long as she wanted to."

"That was impossible. She'd grown old and her fits of cleaning were getting out of hand."

"I've never heard of anyone being bothered by a clean house."

"She tried to keep the boy from sleeping with me in my bed," he answered.

"It's absolutely not necessary for the boy to sleep with you, Johann."

"Dora, she didn't try to keep him away from me because of the dirtiness but because of her jealousy."

Michael's grandmother laughed, full of disbelief.

"You don't understand. I'm giving him the key."

Full of amazement, the grandmother was silent for a moment. Then she said, "Didn't you give it to one of the children?"

"No. Not one of them has inherited the gift."

Michael could swear that his grandmother became purple with rage.

"I can't believe it! After the business with Jeanette, we agreed that you'd give it to one of our children and to no one else!"

"I brought Michael here so that you could see him, to show you that he's worthy of it. He's your grandson too, Dora!"

"The son of that street musician, of that good-for-nothing?"

Suddenly Michael understood that his grandmother had not loved his father. He thought that was awful. "My father's not a street musician, he's the leading cellist in the orchestra!" he wanted to shout, but no sound came from his throat.

In the meantime, the grandmother from the photographs bent over him and shouted, "That'll never happen!"

Michael began to be afraid. He was truly paralyzed and could not offer her any resistance. She searched his clothes feverishly. Then his grandfather came between them and they fell on the floor. The grandmother underwent a metamorphosis that made her unrecognizable. Suddenly she became a monster just like the gruesome figures in nightmares. His grandfather grabbed Michael by the arm and together they fled down the stairs. She fluttered after them until they came to the door. Michael tried the handle, but the door was locked.

"The key!" shouted his grandfather.

Michael opened his hand, but the key had disappeared.

"Open the door, Michael," shouted his grandfather.

"Grandpa, the key is gone!" cried Michael. He tried to push the door open by force, but it was a big, heavy wooden door and it was well locked.

The grandmother fluttered close behind them and stretched two long transparent arms toward them.

"Grandpa, wake up!" cried Michael.

"I can't wake up, I've lost the power over the dream," cried the grandfather. "Can you perhaps wake up and then wake me up?"

Michael tried. He had no idea how to wake up when you are dreaming that you want to wake up.

The grandmother threw herself at Michael, but his grandfather turned over and pulled Michael and his grandmother apart resolutely.

"Go back to your place, Dora! Michael is getting the key!"

Michael could not breathe from fright, and he woke up. He was not completely awake but awake enough to be able to feel the sheet he was lying on with his hands. He found the key, ran to the door, and pushed it into the lock. The door opened.

The next morning Michael looked at the key closely. It was made of iron, but there was no rust on it. It was fairly small and had a bit on both sides. There was nothing unusual about it until his grandfather said that he should hold it against his ear. For the key could sing. It was the singing of the whales.

"Grandpa, what will you do without the key?"

"I needed it only when I was young," said the grandfather. "It's been engraved in my soul for years."

"Who gave it to you?"

"My father. He knew that I had the gift of dreaming, just as he did. And you have it too, Michael."

As Mr. Hammermann's health worsened, his dreams changed. They were not adventures anymore, not journeys through breathtakingly beautiful scenery, but memories, memories that Michael shared as a stranger who had become involved by chance. Sometimes it was exciting, sometimes really scary. There was a very beautiful girl there. She stood opposite a slight young man, and Michael knew that that was his grandfather. Everything was covered in snow, the palm trees and the old city walls of Jerusalem. The two stood arm in arm with their heads leaning against each other. Perhaps his grandfather was able to take the people he loved with him into his dreams even then, Michael thought, surprised. They remained standing for a long time. It started snowing again and Michael collected a big handful to make into a ball. His hands were ice cold and he woke up. He jumped out of bed and ran along the hall to the small light. He looked at his hands closely. The snow had not yet melted, and Michael licked it just as he had licked the snow that had fallen years before. His grandfather called to him. He walked back and showed his hands to his grandfather.

"They're wet."

"No, Grandpa. Snow!"

The grandfather turned on the lamp next to his bed. He looked at the last flakes, which quickly changed into drops of water, and he smiled at them the way you smile at memories. Afterward, he asked Michael to wake up the nurse. She had to bring out the electric blanket and lay it on his legs, for they were ice cold. In actual fact, it was still summer.

Everything seemed to go on as usual, but one morning Michael woke up in his parents' bedroom. His mother was sitting by the bed.

"What am I doing here, Mommy what has happened?"

"I don't know," said the mother. "You and Grandpa weren't in the house anymore and you were found on the street unconscious. What were you doing outside? How could Grandpa have walked so far?"

"I can't remember," said Michael. "Where is he now?"

"He's fine. Later on, when you feel better, you can go to see him for a while."

Michael closed his eyes. He remembered what had happened. They had been back to Grandfather's old house, but the house was not the same as he remembered it. It had only two floors, and in front of the house there was a dirt track instead of a street. There were a few large palm trees in front of the house, although Michael had absolutely no recollection of any palms there. The surrounding city was quite different too. There were only a few houses scattered about. Nothing blocked the view of the walls to the Old City. It was very dark outside and it was dark inside the house too, apart from a few candles that burned in the hall. They walked up the steps, but before they had reached the door, they could hear the sound of hooves and the clatter of a carriage that was approaching jerkily over the uneven road. His grandfather grabbed him by his sleeve. They walked quickly along the road again and hid behind a small wooden building. The carriage came along and stopped. A man wearing a long coat and a top hat stepped out and walked to the door. He knocked. He did not notice that two strangers had come out of the darkness and were creeping up on him from behind. Michael's grandfather ran after them up the steps and shouted in a child's voice, "Daddy!"

Then everything darkened.

That evening Michael sat with his grandfather and asked a lot of questions.

"Was that your father, Grandpa?"

"Yes, Michael, and perhaps I saved his life!"

"Were they robbers?"

"Yes. At the beginning of the century, it was dangerous to go outside after sunset. Most people sought refuge inside the walls of the Old City, and those who lived outside the walls locked themselves in their houses.

"But that night, I'd done something that was strictly forbidden. I'd gone outside to wait in the dark for my father."

"How did you know, Grandpa?"

"Through the key."

After that dream, Mr. Hammermann did not leave his bed again.

Michael visited him every day when he came home from school.

"Grandpa, how do you feel?"

"Not so good. Sit down, read me something from the newspaper."

And every evening Michael gave his grandfather a good night kiss. With his eyes closed he reminded Michael of dead people in television films. Even so, Michael was not sorry he had persuaded his grandfather to get rid of the machine that could make time stand still.

They flew on bicycles above beautiful mountain scenery. Something was dragging on Grandpa's bicycle all the time.

"What a strange spot," the grandfather said when they landed on a dark night between tall trees. They stepped off their bicycles and walked slowly toward the house that stood between the trees. The entrance was lit and the door stood open. A few steps led to the entrance, and through the open door you could see into one of the rooms. Immediately Michael recognized it again. This time too, people were sitting on the stairs, by the entrance, in the room behind the front door, and in front of the window.

"Grandpa, we've been here before."

His grandfather nodded. He was very pale. Then the people called him to come inside. They did not say a word and made no gestures, but the look in their eyes said everything.

Grandfather's bicycle collapsed and was sucked into the ground, which was covered in pine needles.

"Michael, I haven't got a bicycle anymore, and I can't manage to wake up!"

"Grandpa," cried Michael, "don't wake up! You mustn't wake up now!"

His grandfather looked at him intently. "All right," he said.

"Grandpa," said Michael, and he burst into tears.

Mr. Hammermann's funeral took place in actual reality. There was a big crowd of people. When they lowered the coffin into the ground, Michael's mother threw her arm around him. But Michael stood for a while with the key against his ear and had no worries. He knew his grandfather was dreaming now, the dream about the house that was lit up between the dark trees, and he knew that he could always visit him as long as he could find the spot. He definitely had to go there again to see him and to tell him a few things. And first of all, Michael wanted to tell him that Madame Sibonnier was at the funeral and that after the gravediggers had filled in the grave she had dropped down onto the pile of earth, crying.

The members of the family, all kinds of old men and women who had come there from far away, had shaken their heads with a smile which had a touch of understanding as well as a touch of malice. Michael smiled to himself too, because for some reason or other he could not help thinking about his grandfather's meaningful wink again. At the end of the ceremony, Madame Sibonnier came up to his parents to shake their hands, and she bent over to embrace him. Michael endured the embrace, which gave him a warm sensation. Afterward, he pressed the key to his ear again to continue listening to the singing of the whales and to decide that he would become an antique dealer when he grew up, just like his grandfather.

Jordi Sierra i Fabra

Uninvited Guests

1

It was a heartrending shriek.

When she went into his room five seconds later, he was sitting up in bed, his eyes bulging. He was perspiring and his whole body shook. Even in the half-dark bedroom, she saw immediately that he was completely shattered and that it would not be long before he reached total panic. He did not respond until she came and sat next to him on the bed. He clung to her with both hands.

"Mommy! Mommy!"

"Take it easy, I'm with you now, take it easy."

"They're here again, they won't go away. I really want them to go away. Make them go away, please, please!"

She held him tightly, stroked his head with her hand, and rocked him in her arms. She tried to overcome her own sadness. It was almost unbelievable. She had sat still next to him for two hours until he had fallen asleep, exhausted. Peace seemed to have returned. But the moment she wanted to walk out of his room . . .

She was overtired herself, and after all these days she badly needed rest too.

"Mommy, I'm so frightened."

"Tomorrow we'll go to another doctor."

"That won't make any difference. He won't believe me either and he'll give me sleeping pills again, just like the other doctor. I just want someone to take them away from here." He hit his head with his hands. "They must go! They must go, Mommy!"

She held him tighter. She was not capable of doing anything

anymore. She felt just as much pain as her son. They both looked like ghosts, like walking corpses with vacant looks and pale faces because they had not had enough sleep.

Slowly but surely, it was driving them mad.

"Tomorrow, Jorge, I promise you tomorrow," she whispered in his ear. "Dr. Puig is a different kind of doctor. He'll make you better, I'm sure he will. He'll make you better, darling, so that you can sleep peacefully again."

"But if it doesn't help this time either . . . ?"

"Ssh, quiet now!"

"Mommy . . . "

"Sssh."

She still had her arms round him lovingly and she still held him tight.

They both knew it would be another long night.

2

Before Dr. Puig closed the door to his study, he glanced quickly at the little boy with sunken eyes sitting on a bench in the waiting room. He seemed afraid and alone. He looked terrible, just like his mother. You could see that he was very worried about something, that something was really bothering him and that he had hardly slept.

When the boy's mother seated herself before him, the doctor proceeded immediately. He already knew the case history. He just wanted a few more facts, and he wanted to create a pleasant atmosphere so that the boy could settle in and feel at ease.

"Tell me about it."

"Doctor," she began but she burst into tears immediately.

"Please, Mrs. Antich. In these cases, you must try to remain calm, it's almost as important as the treatment itself."

"Yes, doctor, but all these terrible days and sleepless nights . . . "

"When did the problem start?"

"A week ago. It's kept us awake for eight nights now," said Jorge's mother after she had calmed down a little.

"And you've already been to see a doctor?" he went on.

"Yes, after three nights without sleep, I was afraid. But the sleeping pills and the other things they've prescribed for him haven't helped. The sedatives help him fall asleep, but the nightmares just continue. As soon as he falls asleep, they start again. Falling asleep is no problem, the problem is what happens when he's asleep, what is inside his head."

"And you think that that's the case, Mrs. Antich?"

"That there's something inside his head?"

"Yes."

"I don't know."

"But your son says that there are strange creatures inside his head, isn't that so?"

"Yes, that's correct."

"And you believe that?" he asked again.

The woman looked at him. A veil of tiredness and fear hung before her eyes. She did not answer the doctor's last question. She could not.

There was a moment's silence.

"What does your son say exactly?"

"That the creatures come out as soon as he falls asleep. He says they're always inside his head but that they are quiet during the day and at night too, when he's awake. They're only active when he closes his eyes and falls asleep. Sometimes they talk to him."

"What do they say then?"

"That he must just continue sleeping, that he shouldn't resist because there's no point in doing so. Jorge keeps on saying that there are hundreds of them, thousands of them, and that they're small and run round like ants. He says he can feel them but especially . . ."

"Go on," the doctor encouraged her when he noticed she was hesitating.

"Jorge says that he can feel them draining him, that they are pushy and search through everything and take all his memories with them. And he claims that they enter his body too."

"How?"

"When he can't go on any longer, for human beings simply can't go on for days on end without any sleep, when he almost faints or when the sedatives are starting to work, that's when they start moving. He says that not only do they take all kinds of information from him but also that they penetrate his body by way of his arteries and they search through everything. Everything, his heart, his stomach, his liver, his kidneys, everything. Afterward, when he wakes up, he can't move anymore. He just lies there rigid, just as if . . . just as if they've stolen his soul!"

"That's what he tells you?"

"Yes, that's what he calls it, his soul! His being, his real self!"

Dr. Puig leaned back in his chair and folded his hands in front of his face as if he wanted to pray. Opposite him, the boy's mother began to cry bitterly again. She was afraid that Jorge would be driven mad. The doctor was thoughtful enough to wait a moment until Mrs. Antich had calmed down a little.

"When exactly did your husband die?" he asked, in order to open a new topic of conversation.

"It will be two years next month."

"And father and son . . . ?"

"They were very close, yes. Although in the months following his father's death, Jorge recovered extremely well. Children are very good at that. They're full of high spirits and can push away unpleasant things more easily."

"But sometimes, they hide their unpleasant memories somewhere inside their heads. And they can reappear at the most unexpected moments."

"Could it have something to do with my husband's death?"

"It could be that there's a connection. The human soul is very complicated. For example, certain fears and problems can make our bodies sick by means of what is called the psychosomatic process."

"But Jorge keeps talking about strange creatures."

"Does your child indulge in fantasies a great deal?"

"Not more than other children."

"Does he believe in ghosts and monsters? Has he ever been troubled by nightmares before?"

"No, I don't think so."

"Does he play video games?"

"No."

"Does he read a lot?"

"Yes, he reads a lot, but not that type of book."

"What does he enjoy doing?"

"The things that all children like doing at that age—playing football, watching television, nothing special." She gestured with her open empty hands as if she wanted to make it clear that nothing else was wrong. That she could think of nothing else.

"Difficulties at school?"

"No."

"Do you punish him often or do you ever hit him?"

"No!"

"Sorry, but I must examine all the possibilities," explained the doctor, "before I start the treatment."

"What kind of treatment do you have in mind?"

He told her exactly what he planned to do. "I'm going to talk to him first and then I'm going to hypnotize him."

The woman stiffened and looked at him, shocked. She thought she knew vaguely what Dr. Puig was talking about.

"You needn't be afraid," he reassured her. "Hypnosis is often used. You just have to make sure that you have everything under control. It can be a good method of examining a patient's subconscious. If your son has something inside his head or thinks there's something inside his head, we can try to find out what that is exactly and then how we can get rid of it. Sometimes it's so easy that we only have to hypnotize a person to be able to tackle the problem."

"But if you let him go to sleep, it could come back again, couldn't it?"

"I won't put him to sleep. Jorge will remain conscious. You needn't be afraid."

"And if it fails?"

Dr. Puig smiled at her now. With that smile he wanted to cheer her up a little. "We mustn't move too fast, Mrs. Antich! In this case, the main thing is the fight your son is having against insomnia, which is robbing him of sleep that he badly needs. That's very serious. We must do something about it quickly, but we must first try to analyze his case in a sensible way. Jorge has an unusual problem but, in my professional opinion, I think it'll be less difficult to solve than it would appear at first. It can be compared to an item of clothing with a dirty spot. If you wash the item of clothing, well, the spot will disappear completely. I'm now going to try, in a manner of speaking, to be the soap that is going to be used to wash your son's soul. I'm an outsider, and using a hypnosis treatment, I'll probably succeed. He is, when all is said and done, only a child, and children are very receptive and approachable."

"Have you ever had experience with a case like this before?"

He had expected that question. He wanted to be honest with her. "No, I've never had experience with anything like this before. But I'm a doctor, and furthermore I'm a psychiatrist. I understand my profession. If that weren't the case, you wouldn't be sitting here. Shall we start now?"

3

"What's your name?"

"Jorge."

"Can you hear me clearly?"

"Yes."

"Are you comfortable?"

"Yes."

"Are you still awake?"

"Yes."

"Do you feel calm?"

"Yes."

"Can you feel something strange inside your head?"

Silence.

"Jorge?"

"Yes."

"I asked you if you could feel something strange inside your head."

"No, not at the moment."

"Why do you say that, 'at the moment'?"

"Because I'm awake now, I know that, and then they keep quiet."

"Are they there?"

"Yes."

"How do you know?"

"I know."

"And if I should go inside your head, Jorge?"

Silence.

"Would you agree to that?"

Another short silence. "Yes."

"But would they agree to it?"

"I think so. I'm much bigger."

"Then I'd like to go inside and I want you to feel me inside your head. Because I don't want to talk to you from the outside but from the inside. Because I'm your friend, do you understand? I'd like to help you so that you won't have to worry anymore. All right?"

"All right."

"All right," the doctor repeated.

Jorge lay with his eyes wide open, looking at a spot on the ceiling. Dr. Puig now began to speak in a soft, warm voice, even though the patient was responding well to the hypnosis.

"I'm coming into your head now," he said. "Can you feel me yet?"

"I think so, yes."

"You must try very hard to feel me. Can you feel anything?"

"Yes."

"And you must help me. Can you do that?"

"How?"

"I can't see anything, I don't know the way inside there. Where are they now?"

"I don't know."

"You don't know?"

"No, I don't know. They're only there when I'm asleep, aren't they?"

"What happens exactly when you're asleep?"

"Well, then they come out."

"Where do they come from?"

"I don't know."

"But where did they use to live?"

"In their own world, of course."

"What world is that?"

"Baitian."

"Baitian?"

"Baitian," said Jorge once again.

"And where is that, Baitian?"

"Somewhere a long way off in the universe."

"How did you find out their names and the country where they came from?"

"They told me that to keep me quiet."

"How did they get here and how did they get inside your head?"

"With a ship."

"With what kind of ship?"

"With a shadow ship because they are shadows themselves."

"Aren't they creatures with a body?"

"No."

"And why are they inside you?"

"I don't know."

"Are there any more?"

"No, the ones in my head are the only ones, or so they told me."

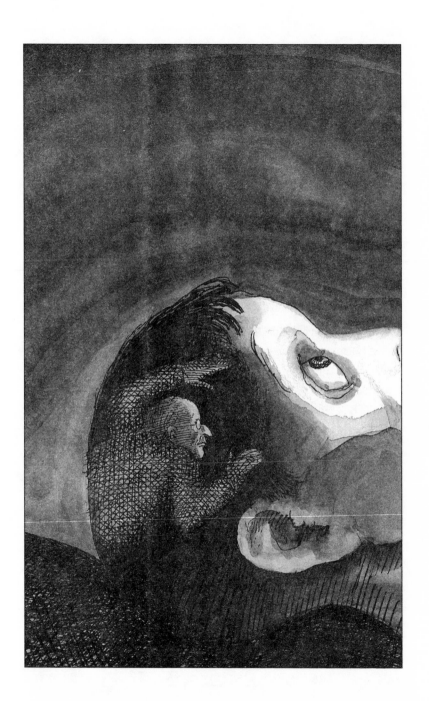

"Why do they want your thoughts, your memories, your soul?"

"That's what they feed themselves with. That's how they live."

How extraordinary that he had invented a construction like this inside himself and in which he believed wholeheartedly, thought Dr. Puig. This was a good moment to tackle the problem or at least make some attempt to do so.

"Are you afraid of them?"

Silence.

"Jorge, answer me."

"Yes," he whispered softly, "I'm very afraid of them."

"Afraid of their appearance?"

"I've never seen them. I can only feel them and sometimes I can hear them too."

"Why are you afraid of them?"

"Because they're slowly killing me, I just know that. When they've robbed me of my actual me completely, then I'll die."

"And what will the Baitians do then?"

"I don't know."

He did not want to wait any longer with the decisive question.

"Do you want them to disappear, Jorge?"

The boy answered immediately. "Yes."

"Do you really want that?"

"Yes." He swallowed.

"Jorge, you must feel it, that's very important. Just wanting is not enough, you have to shout and demand that they go away as loudly as you can. I'll ask you one more time. Do you want them to disappear?"

"Yes."

"One more time!"

"Yes . . . yes . . ."

"Louder!"

"Yes!"

"Louder! Shout it out!"

"Yes, yes, yes!"

"You really want them to go away, that's what you want, isn't it?"

"Yes, I really want them to leave!"

"They must leave! Out! Out! Jorge!"

"Out!"

Jorge became agitated and began to perspire and pant. He gasped for breath and began to flail about wildly with his arms as if he wanted to drive away something invisible from in front of his face. The doctor knew that now there was a channel free inside his soul and that this might well be the beginning of his liberation. Jorge really wanted to be freed from his tormentors. This was the best kind of therapy: that he himself wanted to be free. There was nothing more inside him to hold them there.

"Well done, Jorge, well done. Calm down, calm down," said the doctor in a soft calm voice again. "It's clear that that's what you really want; just do it, then. Do it so that—just do it."

"What should I do?"

"Throw them out."

"Now?"

"Now!"

"How?"

"You're the boss inside your own head. If you think they should disappear, then they can't stay any longer. You must say to yourself, 'I've had enough!' That's enough because now I'm inside you and I've freed a channel inside your head. Tell them you've had enough; then they'll go away."

"I've had enough?"

"Yes."

"I've had enough."

"Louder."

"I've had enough!"

"Still louder."

"I've had enough!!!"

The doctor did nothing for a moment. He waited a second. Then he took hold of the boy's hand and began to stroke it. Then he stroked the boy's forehead too.

"Now you're free," he said to him.

"But they . . . "

"They've gone and they won't be coming back anymore. Take that from me, Jorge. You'll sleep well tonight. The Baitians can't do anything to you anymore. You are much stronger than they are now."

It was so simple and so easy. Pure autosuggestion. He was still only a child, and that should be enough.

Jorge became calmer and calmer, and at last he was really calm and relaxed.

"Do you feel good, son?"

"Yes."

"I'll count to three and then I'll bring you out of the hypnosis, all right?"

"Yes."

"One."

Jorge's breathing became calmer.

"Two."

A smile.

"Three."

And he came out of the hypnosis.

4

Jorge's mother still felt unsure. It was clear she could not believe it completely.

"And if it happens again tonight . . . ?"

"That could happen," the doctor admitted immediately. "But if I'm not mistaken, he'll be all right. Should he be bothered by nightmares tonight, then we'll repeat the therapy. I believe that Jorge has suffered so very much from all kinds of stress that in the end he started to believe in the strange creatures. Children have such great powers of imagination that they have no difficulty in giving actual form to something that is absurd. In fact, I didn't need to do much. I only told him that he's much stronger than they are and that we opened a door together, made a sort of channel along which the strange creatures left. I gave him some inner support. That wouldn't have worked from outside."

"Dr. Puig, if that is so . . . "

"He is still a child, Mrs. Antich," said the doctor with a smile. "And children of his age can develop very strong fantasies. If they begin to live a life of their own, they can be quite dangerous. I don't doubt that for a minute. But Jorge is strong. Children are strong. It could be that the pain of his father's death is only now beginning to surface and that he wanted to attract your attention. Who can say? There are so many things that can be of influence. Watch him carefully during the coming weeks and make sure you stay near him."

"I'll do that."

"Yes, of course," he said with a smile, for he also knew that he need not have said that to her.

"Thank you, doctor," she said and held out her hand. He shook her hand and opened the door for her. Jorge was sitting in the room reading a science fiction comic about astronauts and strange monsters.

"Do you feel okay?" the doctor asked him.

"Yes, sir," said the child.

"I wish you all the best," the doctor said to him.

And when Jorge walked outside with his mother, he closed the office door behind him and smiled.

5

He opened his eyes and lay still, waiting. Nothing.

And it was no dream. He had really just woken up and that meant that . . .

He looked round calmly. The light in his room was on, but he could see through his window that it was already morning, and it had certainly been so for a few hours.

The whole night.

So he had slept all night.

Uninterrupted, peacefully, without nightmares.

He turned his head to one side. His mother was lying next to him on his bed with her clothes on. She was also making up for all those sleepless nights, and, he did not want to wake her. He sat up. At that moment, she woke up in fright. She opened her eyes and looked at him. He thought he saw an anxious, worried look in her eyes again, but with a few words he took away her fear and pain.

"They've gone."

"What did you say?"

"They've gone, Mommy. They're not inside my head anymore."

"Jorge, really?" She could hardly believe her ears. Her son

nodded his head. She could see by his face that it was true—and not only had he slept well, but the creatures had disappeared from his head.

"Oh, son!" She held him tight, so happy that she could laugh again at last. "Darling, my darling!"

"That doctor made them disappear, Mommy! He really made them disappear from my head. And they're never coming back!"

They remained in each other's arms for a minute or two. Then he pulled himself away from her hug and looked at her, frowning, not really afraid, more anxious.

"I wonder where they are," he mumbled worriedly.

"That doesn't matter anymore, does it," said his mother while she stroked his cheek with her hand. "Wherever they are, they can't do you any harm anymore. That's over for good."

"Yes, Mommy, over for good," he said, blissfully happy but still dead tired. "Over for good, although . . . ." He crawled close to his mother again and sighed deeply. "But they must have gone somewhere."

6

Dr. Puig staggered into the bathroom and looked at himself in the mirror. At that moment he felt a blow. It was as if his mind was being crushed in one stroke, which led to the dreadful realization that he was being overcome by enormous panic. What he now saw, he would never have thought possible.

He saw himself in the mirror, but he was changed, almost unrecognizably so. A pair of glassy eyes looked at him, cramped with fear and full of horror. And that after only one night.

"My God," he stammered, full of horror. He tried again, a long way from his bed and standing up straight.

After all, it had been morning for a long time now. Perhaps . . . He closed his eyes.

Just for a second.

"We're here," sang a voice in his head. And it was not only one voice. In that one second, he felt how they ran up and down and picked at his brains and sucked out all his emotions and feelings.

He opened his eyes again.

Yes, of course they were there. They.

And he knew they would stay there for a long time, perhaps too long. For one single hour with Baitians in your head was enough for the rest of your life.